Celibates &
Other Lovers

Celibates &
Other Lovers

Walter Keady

MacMurray & Beck
Denver / Aspen

Copyright © 1997 by Walter Keady
Published by:
MacMurray & Beck, Inc.
1649 Downing Street
Denver, Colorado 80218

Printed and bound in the United States of America

1   2   3   4   5   6   7   8   9   10

Library of Congress Cataloging-in-Publication Data
Keady, Walter, 1934–
Celibates & other lovers : a novel / by Walter Keady.
          p.   cm.
          ISBN 1–878448–77–3
          I. Title.
          PS3561.E16C4   1997
813'.54—dc21   97–15559
                                        CIP

MacMurray & Beck Fiction; General Editor, Greg Michalson
Celibates & Other Lovers cover design by Laurie Dolphin,
interior design by Stacia Schaefer.
The text was set in Sabon by Lyn Chaffee.

TO

Patricia Anne
Aunt Mary
Grace Elizabeth
And to my parents, who would have been proud

ACKNOWLEDGMENTS

I owe undying gratitude to Nancy Willard, without whose encouragement and practical help this book might never have been published. To the Southern Dutchess Writers' Group I owe more than I can say for their friendship and constructive criticism. Many thanks to Diane Sterling for finding me a wonderful publisher. I am forever obliged to Frederick Ramey and the staff at MacMurray & Beck for their enthusiasm, kindness and faith in me. And thank you, Carolyn and Paul, and many other friends—you know who you are—for your unfailing encouragement and support.

The

Vocation

of

Phelim

O'Brien

PHELIM was saving hay back in the long meadow when the word came. The meadow bordered the gravel road that ran between Creevagh and Kilsaggart, and he ever after had a picture in his mind of Bernie walking his bicycle slowly up the steep hill that gave Knockard its name.

"God bless the work." The postman came to a halt at the top and leaned on the bike to catch his breath; he was getting on a bit, in years and in weight. "'Tis a great day for the hay." And indeed it was: after weeks of rain, they had finally gotten a spell of sun and wind.

"Thanks be to God." Michael O'Brien, Phelim's father, kept on raking.

"I have a letter for you," Bernie shouted at Phelim, and the lad dropped his rake and came running. But, although he had been waiting in anxious dread for weeks to hear something, he stood there staring at the white envelope until the postman got back on his bicycle. Bernie's gossip habit was a source of gossip itself in a community that thrived on word-of-mouth news. "Will you stand back and give me air," he yelled at his two brothers and three sisters who had also downed rakes and come galloping up. Michael O'Brien went on with his work.

"Is it what I think it is?" Josephine whispered in his ear. She was the oldest, just a year ahead of Phelim, and the only one of them who knew what he was up to.

"It is." He tried to keep the excitement out of his voice. "They're taking me."

By Sunday the whole parish of Creevagh knew that Phelim O'Brien of Knockard was going to become a priest. It was the summer of 1945, that most wretched hiatus of modern history between the extermination of Adolf Hitler and the surrender of Hirohito. The lad's decision was not a sudden one. And it was not the least bit influenced by the cataclysmic events of the time. Those world-shaking convulsions, terrible as was the recounting of them in the daily pages of the *Irish Independent*, were to Phelim O'Brien insignificant compared to the catastrophe that threatened his own immortal soul if he failed to answer the Divine Call.

A big-boned lad, the same Phelim. With brains to burn: Mr. Addis Emmet, who taught him for five years before sending him to the Christian Brothers in Kilmolara, said he was the brainiest boy who ever entered Creevagh National School. A reluctant admission from the schoolmaster, who still had aspirations for his own wild son, Philpot.

Phelim had the added misfortune of being terribly good-looking. If you were a sparrow in the rafters of Creevagh church on a Sunday morning you might be able to count the number of girls who were sneaking surreptitious peeks at him coming back down the aisle from Communion. Not that it did them any good, mind you, other than the momentary pleasure of it. For Phelim was a fearfully pious lad. A piety fueled, it may fairly be said, as much by fear as by love. From the age of reason he was obsessed with a morbid terror of hell. And from the age of puberty he was tormented with the near certainty that he would wind up in it. The flesh, you see, that he could not control, goaded by an imagination that, despite his level best attempts, would not stay away from girls and their forbidden parts. The resulting guilt was manifest to his body in headaches and diarrhea and to his soul in alternate longing for and loathing of Saturday night confession. He blamed much of his condition on that first ignorant year of evil delights that had occurred between the onslaught of carnality and his recognition of its wickedness.

That the priesthood was his only salvation was the awful conclusion he had come to by the age of sixteen. And he thanked God devoutly and sadly every day since for the grace to recognize it. Celibacy, protected by a long soutane and a holy countenance, alone could shield him from the fires of lust that barred his way to heaven. And the sooner the better. Even that very Sunday morning going to first mass, when he caught up on Mrs. Maille back the road and she was telling him what a great lad he was entirely to be sailing away as a missionary to pagan lands, he couldn't keep his eyes off her daughter Eileen. The mere sight of that beauty brought thoughts to his mind that if he hadn't turned quickly aside would have kept him from the Communion rail. And then at the church gate red-headed Catherine McGrath showed so much flesh above the knee getting off her bicycle that only a quick forced aversion of the eyes saved him from pleasure so fierce as to be most certainly mortal.

He didn't *want* to be a celibate, for God's sake. What sane lad would who ever daydreamed of cuddling gorgeous Eileen in the natural state, or of stroking flaming Catherine's soft skin on those parts he ought not to imagine? But he must choose eternal good over fleeting pleasure. It was Father Coyne taught him that bit of wisdom from the pulpit of Creevagh church. And the Christian Brothers and the Missionaries convinced him that failure to be celibate was tantamount to leaping feet first into the pit of hell.

He took a bit of joking from the lads about his vocation that Sunday morning, as was to be expected. Paddy Moran and Seamus Laffey and his own younger brother Matty, who always knelt at the back and were out of mass first, were waiting for him at the gate.

"No cursing now, lads," said Paddy Moran loudly. "Here comes his reverence."

"You'll be able to go to confession at home now," Seamus Laffey told Matty.

But it wasn't the lads' leg-pulling that bothered him. It was the sight and sound of Catherine McGrath, who came down the church steps just behind him.

"Hello," she said, ignoring the other lads entirely. "What's this I hear about you?" She had a low, soft voice that could drown the strictures of his conscience and a delicately featured face that could, and often did, eclipse the Sacred Heart Itself.

"Nothing terrible, I hope." He tried to be calm. They were friends, he and Catherine. A courting couple, some of the lads said, because they were both from Knockard and they had cycled together every morning into Kilmolara for the past five years, he to the Christian Brothers and she to the nuns. But how could they be courting and they only eighteen years of age? And never so much as exchanged a kiss, for God's sake.

"I suppose we can't even look at you now anymore." She was staring off into the distance herself as if the mere sight of him would be sinful.

"You can look at me anytime you like," Paddy Moran blurted. Catherine ignored him.

"I don't suppose we could entice you to one more dance before you go." She looked at him then and smiled, almost sadly, still with that faraway look.

He knew well that he shouldn't, but he said he might. What else could he say? Especially with the lads there listening.

"We'll see you there then tonight." And she flashed an expanse of white inner thigh while getting on her bike that almost cost him the state of grace.

"We'll see you there then tonight," Seamus Laffey mimicked. "What do you have, O'Brien, that I don't?"

"He went to the Christian Brothers," Matty the brother said, and you might have detected a touch of the crab-apple in his tone, "while the rest of us went to the cowshed."

"He has a willie that he's never going to use now,"

Paddy Moran added sourly. Paddy had a great eye for the girls himself, but he was afraid they wouldn't go for him because, at eighteen, he was already going bald.

"Easy now!" Seamus Laffey raised a half-serious hand. "He's a holy man already, you know." Seamus had thought about the priesthood himself one time, but since he didn't get to go to the Christian Brothers to do his Leaving Certificate, he knew he had no chance. Besides, he was in love with Eileen Maille, though the beauty of Turloughmor didn't know about that yet.

Phelim walked away from them and went back home alone. They were threatening to become an occasion of sin with their dirty talk. Paddy Moran had a habit of saying things. And it wasn't Phelim's fault that he had secured a secondary education and they hadn't. Or that he was better-looking and the girls liked him. For all the good it was doing him anyway. He had pains in his stomach all afternoon thinking about the dance. First he was going because he had promised and you must always keep a promise. Then the Sacred Heart said, What if your going offends Me? Will it? he asked, and It reminded him that Catherine McGrath always danced so close her forbidden parts were touching him. So he said in that case he'd better not go. But his mind wouldn't stay away from Catherine. Not bad thoughts, mind you, just the need to see her and hear her and dance with her one more time.

He sat on the stone wall that separated the yard from the kitchen garden, pretending to be reading a book. He wouldn't go back to Creevagh with Matty and John to play football because he had to stay close to the turf shed that housed the latrine. His mother came out a couple of times and asked if he was feeling well and said he might catch cold and reminded him with something like a tear in her eye that in just four weeks' time he'd be off to the novitiate and he wouldn't want to be sick for that, would he? But except for a couple of trips to the turf shed he stayed on the wall till tea was ready, and after that he helped his brothers with the milking.

It was Josephine made up his mind for him about the dance. She wanted to go and wouldn't be let unless he went with her. So he agreed; reluctantly, he told himself; and for the last time, he told the Sacred Heart. And he rashly promised he'd stay away from Catherine McGrath. But he danced with her anyway. There was a lady's choice early on, and brazenly over she came to the men's side and asked him out. Which caused no end of envious tittering among the lads he was with. A very stuck-up lady, the same Catherine, they used to say, because she kept them all at a distance except for himself.

It was a slow waltz and she didn't say much, just held him tight with her face close to his and the soft points of her breasts touching his chest. He said little either as they shuffled slowly around the floor in a bemused, impure carnal embrace. Banished for the nonce the scolding voice of Sacred Heart and conscience.

"So you're really going to go," she murmured eventually.

"Yes." Though at that very minute he would have let his soul go straight to hell before he'd forfeit the pleasure of her touch.

"Aren't you going to miss all this?" She squeezed closer to him.

"God help me, I am!"

Catherine McGrath tightened her hold and whispered ever so softly, her lips touching his ear, "Then why do you have to go?"

"It's my vocation," he managed, almost blubbering. But his tortured body screamed that he couldn't possibly have such a thing. And he danced with her for the rest of the night, the state of grace forfeited and the protests of the Sacred Heart drowned by the roar of lust and the soft whisperings in his left ear.

So in mortal sin he saved hay and tied oats all the next week. Till on Saturday night he confessed. Father Coyne listened patiently to his litany of sins, the same ones he heard from the same lad almost every week. Bad thoughts eleven times. All of them had to do with Eileen Maille, Catherine McGrath being too close for bad thoughts. He didn't tell all this to Father Coyne, of course, just the essentials. Impure touches; all of them caused by Catherine's pressing breasts in the slow dances and thrusting pelvis in the tango. Bad acts, which the books on purity called nocturnal emissions, but for which he felt guilty because they were brought on by all the bad thoughts. Did you touch yourself? asked Father Coyne, and he admitted he did a few times. The priest whispered that holy purity was a great virtue and we must strive every day to attain it and ask the Blessed Mother for help. And say the rosary once for your penance and a good act of contrition.

He almost cried with relief coming out of the box. And on Sunday after Communion he promised the Sacred Heart he would never, ever sin again. But on Sunday night he danced one more time with Catherine

McGrath and was in the state of sin again for the rest of the week.

Michael O'Brien sold two sheep at the Kilmolara fair to pay for his son's trousseau: a black suit and a black tie and a soutane and six white shirts and two black trousers and a lot of underwear and pajamas and a black hat and two Roman collars. Mickey Mulroe, the tailor on Glebe Street, said he'd have the soutane and the suit and the black trousers ready in time for the lad's departure on September the first and to come in for a fitting one week before. The morning of the fitting, when everyone else had gone out to stook oats, Phelim told his mother, and she standing at the kitchen table with a head of cabbage in her hand, that he wasn't going to the novitiate.

"You're not going?" Nellie O'Brien put the cabbage on the table and wiped her hands on her apron. "What in heaven's name are you talking about?"

"I don't think I have a vocation."

"Jesus, Mary, and Joseph!" She turned her back on him and leaned on the table with both hands and rocked back and forth for a full minute. Then she turned to face him, and there was anger in her eyes. "You've had a vocation now, by your own telling, for the past two years at least. So where in God's name did it suddenly disappear to?"

"I don't know," he said, bending over with the pain in his stomach. "I think it's gone."

"You think!" She was shouting now. "You think! Where did it go to? A vocation isn't like a penny that falls through a hole in your pocket, you know."

He said nothing. Any minute now he was going to have to make a run for the turf shed.

"Someone has been telling you something," Mrs. O'Brien said shrewdly. "And that's the devil's work, let me tell you."

Still Phelim said nothing. He leaned on the dresser with his head bent and his legs close together. His mother's loud certainty was adding to his pain by raising doubts about his latest decision. What if she was right and this was all a temptation from the devil?

"And I bet I know who it is, too. She's no good, that one. No good at all. And you'd do well to stay far away from her." She picked up the butcher knife from the table and sliced the cabbage in two.

"I don't know what you're talking about," he mumbled. And made a mental note that he'd have to confess that lie on Saturday night.

"Back with you then right away and talk to Father Coyne. Explain to *him* what happened to your vocation." She chopped the cabbage into four more pieces. "And after your father selling two good wethers to pay for your clothes."

He rushed to the turf shed, his mind a burning furze, all smoke and flames and imminent destruction. It was all so clear the way it came to him a while ago when he was doing the milking. The Sacred Heart didn't want him to be unhappy. Of course not, said the soothing squish of milk into the bucket. And he was terribly unhappy at the thought of leaving Catherine McGrath and going to the novitiate. He certainly was, said the warm, smooth teats of the brown-and-white cow. So, therefore, he shouldn't go. What could be simpler than that? What indeed, murmured the cow's warm belly his head was leaning against.

Father Coyne didn't see it that way, of course. He was calm about it, mind you, with none of the mother's knife-wielding fury. But then Father Coyne was calm about most things. A stocky man with steel-gray hair and matching eyebrows and a voice that could range from rolling thunder to a soft wind caressing the leaves. It was the caressing tones he chose for Phelim.

"It is perfectly natural," he said, "to get cold feet at the last minute. I remember well the day I went to Maynooth myself. For a whole long year before, I lived off the excitement that this day would bring. Only to wake that morning with the certainty that I did not belong there. Why, I cannot tell you. I felt unworthy, I suppose. I'd be the laughingstock of the place. I came from a very poor farm down by Nephin Mor. My father had to borrow the money to buy my black suit. So what would a poor lad like me be doing in a grand place like Maynooth? But that was the devil, you see. Trying to trick me out of my vocation. And he's doing the same thing to you now, Phelim. Well, you won't let him, lad, will you? You have spent the last two years praying and thinking about your vocation. And you are dead solid sure that it comes from Almighty God. So the time for thinking about it is over, at least till you have tested yourself in the novitiate. My advice to you now is to pack your bags and off with you to Kilshane." And Father Coyne stood and clapped Phelim on the back and smiled a great warm smile that said, you can trust your parish priest to tell you the will of God. "Write and tell me how you're getting on whenever they let you." And he put his left hand on Phelim's head and raised his right hand in blessing over him and asked his housekeeper,

Mary Hughes, to give the lad a cup of tea and some currant cake before sending him home.

Phelim resolutely put aside his temptation. The parish priest was the voice of God. Might as well contradict the Sacred Heart Itself as fly in the face of Father Coyne's advice. He went to town for the fitting and saw a terribly young priest in a long black soutane looking back at him out of the tailor's mirror. It was a proud moment for him. His mind was made up.

He would be off to the novitiate on Tuesday morning. On the Sunday night before, he impulsively rejected common sense and the sorrowful voice of the Sacred Heart and went off with the lads to one last dance in Kilmolara. "I just want to say goodbye to everyone," was his glib explanation to his mother, and he going out the door.

"Sure you do," she shouted after him with all the sarcasm that helpless wisdom could convey.

"I'm wondering if I really have a vocation," he said to Catherine McGrath during a slow foxtrot, and she clinging to him like he was a wall and she the ivy.

"And why is that?" Not relaxing her grip one iota.

"I don't know if I can leave you." Amazed as he spoke at what was coming out of his mouth. It was the most intimate and personal thing he had ever said to anyone in his entire life. But they were true words if ever he spoke a true word.

"Arrah, go on out of that!" She pulled back without missing a step and looked at him as if he had suddenly gone stark raving mad. "Is it me?" And she giving him this big, innocent smile. "God forbid *I* would ever stand in the way of your vocation. What would people think?"

"I don't know," he said miserably. It wasn't what he expected her to say, for sure. He had been dreaming she'd whisper softly in his ear that her life's happiness depended on him, and then maybe the Sacred Heart might relent and tell him he had better stay home and marry her.

"Phelim O'Brien," she said, "you had better go to that place now and spend at least a couple of months in it or I'll never talk to you again. I mean it. I won't have people saying I'm responsible for stealing your vocation." And she smiled ever so sweetly at him and looked into his eyes in that way she had that turned him into melted butter and then wouldn't dance close to him again for the rest of the night.

On the Tuesday morning at half past nine, wearing his new black suit and tie and carrying a dented blue tin suitcase with leather bands that belonged one time to his deceased grandfather, the Lord have mercy on him, and seen off by his teary-eyed mother and phlegmatic father and bawling sister Josephine, Phelim O'Brien got on the train at Kilmolara en route to the Holy Ghost Novitiate at Kilshane in the County of Tipperary.

A

Most

Respectable

Man

MR. ADDIS Emmet, the schoolmaster of Cree-vagh, was a man of towering respectability. Never mind his stature, which witty estimates by ebriated patrons of Gannon's had put at somewhere between five and eleven inches, though he was as a matter of historical fact exactly five feet four and three-quarter inches in his shiny black leather shoes. Or his lack of hair, which was also humorously commented on by the same Gannon drunks, many of whom were scarcely more hirsute than he. Or even the fastidious elegance of his speech, which from anyone else would be an affront of affectation, the men of Gannon's preferring short words to long.

Mr. Emmet, needless to say, did not frequent Paddy Gannon's pub. And he was not expected to. The men who did tipped their caps to the schoolmaster whenever they met him. And if they occasionally spoke disrespectfully of him while raising a pint to their lips, it was simply the kind of disrespect that was due to a man of higher station from those of lower rank in life. There was nothing whatever in it that reflected on the personal character of the schoolmaster of Creevagh.

Mr. Emmet was proud of his eminent status in the parish, though he would never let on about that. Prouder still was he of his name, a fact he admitted discreetly every year when discussing its historical significance with his sixth class scholars. He would imply on those occasions, though mind you never actually say so explicitly, that he was a descendant of the illustrious man whose name he bore. However, and for good reason, he would never state how that lineage might have occurred. He was the son of Thomas Emmet, a small farmer from Barnadearg who was well versed in the history of both his family and his country. A Catholic with a Protestant name by way of illicit shenanigans in an ancient haystack, Thomas Emmet was in fact a bit of a snob. He might have called his son Robert after the great martyred patriot, but that name, despite its historical renown, offended his sense of the fitting. He was reported as saying when questioned on the subject that "every Tom, Dick, and Harry is named Robert." Instead he endowed his son with the name Addis, the middle name of the illustrious older brother of the martyr.

The parish addressed its schoolmaster respectfully as Mr. Emmet. Except for Father Coyne, of course, who called him Addis. And Tom Graham, the blacksmith, who didn't speak to him at all because of a personal grudge. And Paddy Gannon, who called him Sir to his face and Addis Ababa behind his back.

A great man entirely, everyone said of Mr. Emmet. The acme of eminence in the parish, with the exception, naturally, of Father Coyne himself. And terribly respectable. In a milieu where cow dung was more common on boots than polish, his shoes always shone. Low shoes, of course; not the hobnailed boots of the farmer. And as for the crease in his trousers, "you could cut butter with it," Matty O'Brien, one of the local wags, used to say. He even had a motor car, one of only four that appeared in the parish after the War, when petrol could be had again.

Mr. Emmet's wife, known mostly as Mrs. Addis, or just plain Mrs., was a teacher as well. She taught infants, first and second in Creevagh National School. A quiet woman whom nobody knew and everybody liked. She played the harmonium in church and rehearsed the girls' choir to sing at last mass on Sunday. And sat beside her husband when he drove his shiny black Ford into Kilmolara of a Saturday evening to get the groceries.

The Emmets had only two children, a suspected reproductive failure that gave rise to endless speculation about Mrs. Emmet's capabilities among the women of the parish and about the relationship between brains and masculinity among the patrons of Gannon's. However, in the light of events, maybe two were enough.

Sarah, the oldest, was a bit of a brat who at the age of twelve showed her knickers at the back of the school outhouse to a couple of seventh class lads for the sum of a penny a peek. When rumor of this reached Mr. Emmet, he strapped the lads unmercifully every day for a week and packed Sarah off to a convent boarding school in Kilkenny. It was Philpot Emmet, the son, however, who caused most grief to his parents. It was alleged by some that the father and mother themselves were partly to blame. Saddling the poor eejit with a name like Philpot. Never mind that it belonged to the father of the sweetheart of the great martyred patriot. Anyone with half a brain, or even a slight appreciation of the vulgar, could see immediately the kind of nickname it would spawn. But the parent Emmets, though well endowed with the gray matter, were somewhat lacking in understanding of lower-class humor. And so Philpot Emmet was known, from the first day he started school in low infants' class, as Pisspot. And he was never known as anything else, either in school or in the parish at large. Even years after he had left Creevagh in disgrace.

Philpot, mind you, was a good-natured boy. He felt a great need to be liked, to be one of the lads despite the dual handicaps of being both Pisspot and the schoolmaster's son. And he did succeed in being accepted by his peers, mainly through close identification with them in misery. The father schoolmaster showed no favoritism when it came to using the strap. If anything, he numbed poor Philpot's palms with stinging thwacks for even lesser offenses than other boys. The son in turn showed no pity in pillorying the parent right to his back. A normal young nipper, Pisspot, everyone said. In all respects but one.

There was a powerful libidinous strain passed down in the Emmet family. Very likely from that ancient haystack ancestor. So when it surfaced in Philpot during the early stages of puberty it was remembered by the old-timers in Gannon's that a similar vice had afflicted his great-grandfather, Red Tom Emmet, a farmer with an extraordinary affinity for sheep. It was noticeable, too, to a lesser extent in the grandfather, they said, particularly with reference to the parish priest's housekeeper at the time, though no proof was ever produced, as it were.

That strain was not visible, of course, in the deportment of Mr. Addis Emmet. On the contrary, the Creevagh schoolmaster was sufficiently cognizant of his own moral rectitude to verbally castigate one of his scholars in front of the whole class for the scandalous indiscretions of that scholar's older sister. This occurred, of course, before Mr. Emmet's own children were indiscreet.

"There's bad blood there for sure," Paddy Gannon noted to his customers when young Philpot's first essay in lechery was recounted in the pub. But then no more was said, out of respect for the schoolmaster, until Thomas Ruane indiscreetly raised the subject.

It wasn't a very serious escapade in itself, everyone agreed. But it was a sign of worse things to come, you could be sure of that. Father Coyne, for reasons unknown, decided to take a walk around the back of the church after Benediction one Sunday evening and in doing so came upon Philpot kissing a girl behind a bush. What made the incident most disgraceful was the fact that the lad was a mass-server and was still wearing his surplice and soutane: just moments previously he had been swinging the smoking thurible in homage to the Blessed Sacrament. The girl was a streel, a good-for-nothing slut who had left school two years before and was already putting powder and lipstick on her face.

Needless to say, the parish priest took firm and immediate action. He sent the streel running with a healthy skelp to the backside from the blackthorn he always carried. Then he marched young Philpot, still clad in surplice and soutane, up the village street to the teacher's house, keeping a firm grip on the miscreant's earlobe.

The lad was mortally humiliated because some of the older fellows were still hanging around the church gate before going off to the dance in Kilmolara.

"I only kissed her, Father," he argued, vainly trying to free the tortured ear. "That wouldn't make her foal. Would it?"

Poor Father Coyne was too horrified at this vulgar profanation of the young lad's sacred vestments to vouchsafe a reply.

Mr. Emmet calmly contained his rage out of respect for the priest's presence, confining himself to the promise that he would teach the lad a lesson. Philpot would never divulge afterwards what that lesson was, but it was noted by his peers that for a full week thereafter he never once sat down in school.

Three months later—just a week after Phelim O'Brien went to the Holy Ghost Novitiate—Philpot was sent as a boarder to Mount St. Joseph's College in Roscrea, a secondary school for boys run by the Cistercian monks. He was not quite thirteen years of age.

But if his parents or Father Coyne—or any of Gannon's patrons, for that matter—thought such incarceration would tame the fire in the young libertine's loins, they were sadly mistaken. After four years and three months of strict discipline and grinding studies and unrelenting sporting activities and the most scrupulous indoctrination in the sinfulness of sex in all its nefarious aspects and

A

Most

Respectable

Man

19

disguises, Philpot Emmet came home for the Christmas holidays and got himself into serious trouble.

With the very daughter that Jimmy McTigue had boasted would be up in Dublin in the Civil Service in a few years. Annie May was two classes ahead of Philpot in Creevagh and was going to the convent school in Kilmolara a whole year before he was sent away to the Cistercians. During that year the gallant young rake used to make a point of being early on the road to school so he could watch her pass on her bicycle. On windy days, and most days were windy, her dress would billow, revealing her slim white legs, sometimes all the way up to the knickers. For reasons he was not quite sure of at that stage of his development, the sight gave great pleasure to Philpot. As with most nippers of his time, while nature was on schedule, instruction was tardy. He knew titillation but hadn't been told it was wrong. He was aware, of course, from the age of reason on, of a general principle of theology that if you enjoyed anything it was bound to be evil. But he asked no questions and, until the kissing episode, was given no information on carnal sin.

The lecture his father delivered with the tanning of his hide was, as might be expected, obfuscating rather than enlightening. It compounded shame and disease and blindness and hell into a single great consequence that seemed to the recipient out of all proportion to the committed act. Philpot, whose natural cynicism was reinforced by his upbringing, dismissed it as just another act of parental intimidation. And the delicate dissertations on chastity at Mount St. Joseph's were to him a source of sly humor, even though they were taken with great seriousness by almost all of his classmates. Needless to say, he was never admitted to the college Sodality of the Children of Mary. In his fourth year he did strive mightily for admission, not out of piety but because with the sodality medal went the incongruous and unofficial title of G-Man. To be a G-Man was to be looked up to by the juniors, and even by one's peers when one became prefect of a dormitory or head of a table in the refectory. Philpot's conduct, however, which ranged from illicit smoking in the toilets to a couple of forbidden forays into town—for which he was almost expelled—precluded any possibility of his ever joining that elite corps.

The lad's frame of mind coming out of church with his parents and sister that fateful Christmas morning was somewhat less than pious. He was bored by the three successive masses he had been forced to attend. Inside him the great Emmet libido, after almost four intolerable months without so much as seeing a girl, was chugging restively through his seventeen-year-old veins. And the prospect of spending the next two weeks with the grandma was giving rise to alternate thoughts of murder and suicide. That his holidays were all taken at his maternal grandmother's farm down by the Nephin Mountains was a precaution plotted by Father Coyne and executed by Mr. Emmet to keep him out of trouble. Anyway, the sight of Annie May McTigue standing talking just inside the church gate, gorgeously clad as she was in a bright yellow coat and flaming red hat, set him ablaze like a furze bush in March.

Matty O'Brien, who was an eyewitness, described the scene afterwards to the lads. "Pisspot," he said, "takes off down the steps like a bull after a heifer. Only there's ice on one of the steps and he slips and lands on his backside with his head right between her legs. So Annie May looks down at him and says, 'Philpot, you're looking up my dress again.' And you know what Pisspot says? 'Force of habit,' he says. 'Though I haven't seen your knickers for years.'"

Indeed, Philpot had only occasionally seen Annie May since he went to Mount St. Joseph's. But before he had time to pursue the conversation further, Mr. and Mrs. Emmet were on either side of him. "Will you please get up and not be making a donkey out of yourself," said the schoolmaster with dignified disgust. Philpot's sister was snickering loudly.

"There's a dance in Kilmolara tomorrow night," Philpot said from the ground to Annie May, ignoring his father. "Maybe I'll see you there?"

"Faith, you won't, my lad," said Mr. Emmet. "There'll be no dance for you tomorrow night. Or any other night either. You're going to your grandmother's first thing in the morning."

"I'll see you at the dance, then, Annie May," Philpot said. And he picked himself up and walked away with the utmost dignity. It was about the only trait of his father's that he had inherited.

It was the custom of Mr. and Mrs. Addis Emmet to drive their son to the grandmother's house on St. Stephen's day. They had done so for four years in a row now, ever since Philpot was caught kissing the girl behind the church. But on this particular morning when Mr. Emmet swung the starting handle, there issued from the Ford a single sound like the death rattle of a horse. Then all was silence except for the grunting of Mr. Emmet as he swung and swung without effect.

Young Philpot stood there sphinxlike, suitcase in hand, watching his father's gyrations. When Mr. Emmet finally admitted defeat and said he'd have to go to the post office and telephone Kilmolara for a mechanic, the lad showed no elation at his reprieve. When the schoolmaster returned and announced that the mechanic would not be available for two days, all he said was, "I might as well put the suitcase away for a while, then."

The father looked hard at the son but could detect no sign of triumph. And though he had the strongest of suspicions that the hand of the boy was in the car's incapacity, there was nothing he could prove and so nothing to be charged. He could not resist, however, a parting shot as Philpot went in the door.

"Don't think you are going to any dance tonight, my boy."

Philpot played handball in the ball alley next to the church all that cold, crisp afternoon. When the family said the rosary as usual at nine he yawned great yawns throughout and immediately afterwards went to his room, expressing extreme tiredness. An hour later, when Mr. Emmet was going to bed, he stopped at the boy's door to listen and heard great hearty snoring from inside.

Mr. Emmet was puzzled that his son was sleeping so late the following morning, for the lad was always an early riser. He looked in once with a view to getting him out of bed, but seeing the motionless bundle decided magnanimously to let him sleep a little longer. At about eleven o'clock, when he was out at the side of the house polishing the car, he spotted Jimmy McTigue coming up the road on his bicycle in a great hurry. It was a most unusual sight: Jimmy was a man well known never to be in a hurry about anything. So much so that down at Gannon's the wise ones predicted he would be late for his own funeral.

"Where is that scheming lecherous hoor?" the farmer from Leicaun roared, dropping his bike at the gate and galloping up the schoolmaster's path.

"Hello, Jimmy. How are you?" Mr. Emmet said expansively, pausing calmly from his polishing. Though already his great brain was wondering if there were a connection between the man's agitation and that son of his own still asleep in the bedroom. He was recalling the incident of Christmas morning.

"My Annie May didn't come home from the dance last night," McTigue panted, standing squarely, spread-legged, arms akimbo, in front of the schoolmaster, a stance few men in the parish would have had the temerity to take.

"Did she not now?" Mr. Emmet said, relaxing a little. At least he could vouch for where his son was last night. "I'm sorry to hear that." He wiped a finger where a bit of polish had lodged. "I don't allow Philpot to go to those things," he added in a slightly superior tone. "You get all kinds of riffraff at them, and there's no telling what's likely to happen. You're better off to keep the children at home these days. Particularly the girls, of course."

If Mr. Emmet had been paying any attention at all to the expression on Jimmy McTigue's face, he might have been a lot less supercilious. "Your son, Mr. Emmet," said McTigue, barely able to shout with the effort at breathing, "is the worst kind of riffraff. There is no worse kind of riff and there's no worse kind of raff than your pisspot son. The fooking blackguard was at that dance in Kilmolara last night. And he left it in the company of my daughter. And she hasn't been seen since. And I have come here to find your son. And when I do I'm going to beat the fooking shite out of him until he tells me where my daughter is and what he did to her. Do you understand me, Mr. Emmet?"

There was a menace in McTigue's question that made the schoolmaster step back a pace. But he wrapped his enormous dignity around him and said, "Be calm, my good man. My son was not in Kilmolara last night. He was at home here in bed where he belongs. I made sure of that. As a matter of fact he is still in bed. And I will fetch him to prove it."

So Mr. Emmet escaped into his house, leaving the frantic farmer outside the door. He stormed into his son's room, shook the bedclothes, and shouted, "Get up out of that, Philpot, you lazy good-for-nothing boy. There's someone outside who wants to talk to you."

But just as he ended his speech the uneasy thought came swiftly to him that his son might not be under those bedclothes. His punching and pulling produced only sounds of flatulence and visible deflation till it was clear that unless Philpot had suddenly exploded from excessive gas he could not be underneath. Mr. Emmet ripped off blankets and sheets till he was confronted with nothing but the lad's pajamas and a single solitary unburst balloon.

"I'll kill the bastard," McTigue exploded when Mr. Emmet informed him of the state of affairs. The bastard appellation, however, was an unfortunate indelicacy, even in the heat of such a moment. Mr. Emmet had a very great, and reasonably well-known, sensitivity to the term. For there were those who claimed, and with the backing of wedding and birth chronologies, that Mr. Emmet himself had been conceived in bastardy. Be that as it might, his son, whatever his current infamy, had been born in the most chaste wedlock imaginable, and Mr. Emmet was not about to allow a lout from Leicaun to impugn his virtue or that of Mrs. Emmet.

"By God, if you don't keep a civil tongue in your head, you ruffian, I'll strike you," roared the diminutive Mr. Emmet, his anger for the nonce overriding his much-lauded dignity. Not to mention his prudence, for Jimmy McTigue stood more than six feet tall and was built like a bullock.

"Do so, then," roared back the man from Leicaun. "And I'll kick your fooking bald head from here to Kilmolara. And I'll—"

"What kind of savages are we at all?" The quiet but sharp schoolmistress voice of Mrs. Emmet, standing in the doorway, instantly deflated McTigue's ferocity.

"Sorry, ma'am," he said meekly. "I—"

"I think we had better talk with Father Coyne," Mrs. Emmet said decisively. And neither her husband nor Jimmy McTigue had a word to say while they walked the hundred yards or so down to the priest's house.

"Oh, but he's a right rascal entirely," the parish priest said when he heard the story. They were in the parlor, standing; the situation was too urgent for sitting.

"When I get my hands on him I'll come down on him like a ton of bricks," Mr. Emmet said, rubbing his hands together fiercely as if warming them for the task.

"I'll kick—" Jimmy McTigue began and stopped, his respect for the cloth overriding his righteous anger.

"We had best inform the Gardai," Mrs. Emmet said quietly.

"Yes, yes indeed. We'll do that," Father Coyne agreed. "Addis, you and Jimmy will come with me to Kilmolara."

"They could be anywhere by now," Mr. Emmet said in a distant kind of voice. As if he were no longer among those present. "In Dublin even. And by tomorrow they could be in London. What will we do at all?"

"My girl is ruined for sure," Jimmy McTigue said in a resigned kind of way. "They'll have to get married, of course, Father, won't they?" His tone was anxious, though hardly despairing.

"Good God!" Addis Emmet exclaimed. He put his hands to his face and turned his back on them all and cried. His body was shaking and his sobs were audible, and no one knew what to say or do. Even Mrs. Emmet, who had never seen her husband cry in eighteen years of marriage, stood helplessly looking at his quivering shoulders for several moments. Then she put her arms around him from the back and murmured expressive things like, "There, there, now!" and "Don't cry, dear; things will be all right."

"They won't be all right!" Mr. Emmet exploded, the anger taking over again from the tears. "Bloody fellow! He didn't get it from me." And he glared at Mrs. Emmet, who looked pained but said nothing.

"We'd best go, then," Father Coyne said.

The three men headed for Kilmolara in the parish priest's car. And on the road just outside Creevagh they met Paddy Moran, who admitted to seeing the pair at the dance last night. But no, Paddy had no idea where they might have gone afterwards.

The Gardai of course were most helpful. Garda Kirwin, who was almost a personal friend of Mr. Emmet, spent a full half hour taking down particulars and asking detailed questions about what the pair might have been wearing. He even delicately inquired as to the color and design of Annie May's underwear—"all in the line of duty, Father"—in response to the parish priest's shocked expression. And he would ask for tidings of them at the railway station, he said. There was a morning train from Kilmolara that made a connection at Claremorris with the Dublin train.

When they got back to Kilmolara, Mrs. Emmet was waiting for them at the priest's house. "Philpot is home," she said in her quiet voice. "And he says Annie May is also at home now."

"I'll see both of them here this evening," Father Coyne said sharply. "At my doorstep in an hour."

And they were. Delivered by tight-lipped fathers who left only when the parish priest said, "I'll take care of them now." "The seal of confession is around this door," Father Coyne said when he had them ensconced in his parlor. "Nothing that is said here will pass through it. Do you understand?"

"Yes, Father." Philpot looked defiant. Annie May appeared to have been crying.

"Where were you all night, then?"

They looked at each other. Annie May put down her head. Philpot cleared his throat. "We were at Annie May's grandmother's house," the lad admitted.

"You were, now, were you? And your grandmother let ye stay there all night, Annie May?" There was a hard, incredulous glint in the priest's eye.

"My grannie is in the hospital in Castlebar for the past week," Annie May acknowledged, glancing up timidly at the priest. "She has a touch of pneumonia. I've been taking care of the house for her while she's away." She looked like she was going to cry again.

"I see," Father Coyne said. And he sat there in silence for a while, looking at the table as if it were a chessboard and he was contemplating his next move. "Did you sleep together?"

Philpot glanced first at Annie May, but she kept her head down. Then with those big, innocent brown eyes of his, he looked straight at the priest. "Ah, no, Father, not at all," he said disarmingly. "We never slept a wink all night."

The affair blew over, as those things always do eventually. Philpot was sent back to Mount St. Joseph's to do his Leaving Certificate. Jimmy McTigue blustered for a while to Mr. Emmet that if his daughter got in a family way, there would have to be a wedding. But she didn't and there wasn't. The fellows in Gannon's soon let go of their jokes about Philpot. The sad sight of the father's humiliation—though the schoolmaster, to give him his due, never held his head higher—put a stop to all wit at the creature's expense.

Of course, as regards Philpot, they were just putting their gossip in abeyance. They knew full well they hadn't yet heard the final escapade. Not by a long shot.

A

Most

Respectable

Man

29

The
Cut
of
a
Priest

PHELIM O'Brien came home every summer for a holiday with the family. He stayed exactly a month, arriving on the first of August and leaving on the thirty-first. And every single morning he cycled back to Creevagh to nine o'clock mass, dressed in his black suit and Roman collar.

"Faith, he looks like a priest already," Pat Moloney said to Thomas Ruane one morning. They were going to the bog in Thomas's asscart when Phelim passed them on his way home.

"He has the clothes," Thomas agreed. "And he has the big words, too, begob. But he doesn't have the cut of a priest yet." He hit the ass a skelp with the stick to coax him up the hill.

"I suppose not," said Pat, but you could see by the look on his face that he didn't know what in God's name Thomas was talking about.

"The priest has a bit of mystery about him, you see," Thomas expanded. "He's different that way from the rest of us. A fellow once told me at the fair of Kilmolara that you could tell a priest just by standing near him, even if you couldn't see him. And I noticed it myself about Father Coyne last month at the stations."

"Is that a fact now," said Pat. "Well, on my oath! And what is it do you think that makes Father Coyne different from you or me?"

"Damned if I know now," Thomas said. "But 'tis there all the same. That's the mystery, I suppose. You can feel when you're talking to him that he's more than just a common man."

Phelim O'Brien, cycling slowly home, was feeling not more but less than a common man on that particular morning. For one thing, he almost hadn't gone to mass at all. For another, although he had received Holy Communion he wished now he hadn't, because it was just possible that he was in the state of mortal sin, and a bad Communion was infinitely worse than no Communion at all. And to cap it all, for the first time in his life he truly wished he were dead, which in itself might well be another mortal sin. All because of Reddy Ryan. Catherine McGrath too, of course, but it was mainly Reddy's fault getting him into it. Not that he wasn't partly to blame himself for not letting sleeping dogs lie, as it were.

"They tell me Catherine is getting married," was his

casual remark to Reddy that started the whole chain of events. Back in Mulligan's field on Sunday afternoon, after they finished up a bit of football practice to get the Creevagh team ready for the O'Hara Cup semifinal. His mother had briefly mentioned the upcoming nuptials in a letter last month, but he wouldn't dream of asking anybody at home about it; they might think he was still carrying a torch for Catherine. Which he wasn't at all at the time, even though he did feel a dull pain somewhere in his insides when he got the news. But getting married to Thomas Ryan! The man was old enough to be her grandfather. What on earth had possessed her? So when he got Reddy on his own coming off the field he couldn't resist the urge to learn a little more.

"Don't talk to me about it," Reddy growled back at him. "It would make a dog vomit just thinking on it." And Phelim could see from the look on his face that his friend was in mortal agony.

"Ah, yes! Didn't you have a soft spot for her yourself?" He was remembering how Reddy would be even less talkative than usual whenever she was around.

"Fat lot of good it did me." Phelim could almost taste the sourness in Reddy's tone. "I'm too young for her, I suppose." He put his hand on the wall and jumped over instead of going out through the gap.

"How old is he anyway?" Catherine was only twenty-one, he knew, the same as Reddy and himself.

"My father will be fifty-nine at Michaelmas, and Thomas is a good two years older. He's my godfather, for Christ's sake!" Reddy shouted, then looked around, embarrassed, to see if he had been heard. They were coming up to the gate at the side of Mulligan's Bar, Victuals, and

Grocery, but the rest of the lads were well behind them. "What in bloody hell does she want to marry him for?" Reddy whispered in a tone of terrible pain.

"God only knows," said Phelim, grateful that he himself had long since recovered from his infatuation for the Knockard redhead. A year's novitiate followed by two so far in the scholasticate had cured him of his romantic fancies. He was a professional celibate now and reasonably content with his lot.

"It's the money and the land," Reddy said, and there was great bitterness in his voice. "A power of money came into the place from his wife's cousin who died in America years ago. And now that the wife is dead herself, the Lord have mercy on her, it all belongs to Thomas."

"You think she's marrying him for the money?" It was sad to think of his Catherine, whom he used to be so fond of, being so materialistic. His own vow of poverty, taken at the end of the novitiate, had stifled any desire he ever had for worldly goods. And he was a happier man for that.

"What else? It certainly wasn't for his . . . Never mind." Reddy looked suddenly embarrassed. They walked in silence up to the church gate, where they had left their bikes. "You used to be great friends with her one time," Reddy remembered, tying his togs and boots to the carrier. "I can still see the two of you dancing in Kilmolara. We used to call you the courting couple." But Phelim felt the shyness in his friend's grin. The lads were already treating him with the kind of reverence people reserved for the priest.

"A long time ago and a lot of water under the bridge,"

he said, embarrassed too: he didn't want to be reminded of his foolish behavior three years ago before he went into the novitiate.

"Do you think," said Reddy casually, and they cycling slowly back the road home, "maybe you'd have a word with her?"

"A word with who?" Phelim's mind at that moment was deeply engaged in a bit of worry about the fact that he hadn't yet begun his Little Office for the day. It was five o'clock already, and by this time he should have it all said except for Vespers and Compline. That was the rule, and he must observe it at home the same as in the scholasticate. The football was the distraction: he wanted to play against Ballindine before he went back. But maybe he shouldn't if it was interfering with his spiritual life.

"With Catherine," Reddy said and almost choked. He had to clear his throat a couple of times before he could continue. "I was thinking that maybe if you were to say something to her she might listen. I know she wouldn't pay any attention to a fellow like me but to someone like yourself . . ." Reddy put his head down and cycled fiercely on ahead.

"What would I say to her?" They got off their bikes at the Turloughmor boreen to wait for the other lads. "Dearly beloved Catherine," said Phelim, waving his arms in a rough imitation of Father Coyne in the pulpit, "marry not that ancient codger, Thomas Ryan, with all his land and with all his money. Wed instead this long, this lanky, this half-witted, good-looking young fellow on my right, the one and only Reddy Ryan, the second-greatest footballer in the parish of Creevagh, who doesn't have a penny to his name, mind you, and your reward shall be very great in heaven."

The humor was lost on Reddy. "It would be great now if you would say something like that to her. But you could leave out the bit about me having no money, even if it is true."

"Don't be an eejit, Reddy!" Phelim fairly yelled. The joke had gone far enough. "I can't go back to Catherine McGrath and talk to her about you. I haven't so much as said hello to her for years." It was true. He had avoided her or she had avoided him or God had seen to it that they didn't meet. And that was the way it should be. They went to different masses on Sundays, and of course he didn't go to dances anymore. He did see her once last year when he was walking down Glebe Street in Kilmolara on his way to Mrs. Walsh's bookshop; she came down the opposite side of the street but either didn't see him or pretended she didn't, though he had kept his eyes glued to her till she passed.

"It might make a world of difference if you were to have a word with her," Reddy persisted. "Everyone is saying she's daft to marry him, but no one will say it to her face."

"I can't do it," Phelim said vehemently. Just the thought of it was starting up rumbles of discomfort in his stomach. "It wouldn't be right for me to say anything."

"I'll go down on my bended knees to beg you," said Reddy, and he did, there at the entrance to Turloughmor boreen. And he was so sincere and so desperate that what could poor Phelim say? He said, all right, he might. That was Sunday evening. On Monday evening Reddy was back to the house after milking, and he called Phelim out to the yard to ask in a whisper if he had talked to her yet. He hadn't, of course. The pest came again on Tuesday. On Wednesday he looked so down in the mouth that Phelim promised solemnly he'd go over there Thursday come hell or high water. And he did.

It was in the middle of the afternoon. He told his mother he was going for a walk, which wasn't a lie, because he didn't want her to know where he was going; his mother had no time for Catherine McGrath. He turned in the boreen to her house, hoping there was no one in a field anywhere taking notice. He felt strange walking in the garden path, though he had always been in and out of the place as a nipper. He said, "God bless" over the kitchen half-door and prayed there would be nobody home. Catherine's voice shouted, "You too" from inside. But thank God there was no one there only herself. The rest were back the field stooking oats, she said, taking a pot off the fire and carrying it outside the back door. "And how are you at all, Phelim? It's been a dog's age since we saw you." She was in her bare feet and had no powder or lipstick on, so the freckles were very pronounced and the eyes he looked at only briefly seemed a bit tired. "I'll be going out myself in a little bit; I have to go back to see the dressmaker in Kilmolara."

He couldn't think of a thing to say. He was glad to see her, of course, but he felt as awkward as a newborn calf and half wished he hadn't come. She was terribly reserved, too, not at all the exuberant lass he remembered. It reminded him of the time her mother died, during the first term they were at school in Kilmolara. For a full year after she wore a black patch on her sleeve and wouldn't laugh or smile and would talk only of serious things. Now she asked formally about each member of his family, though he knew she didn't like them very much, especially his mother. And she talked about her own mother, the Lord have mercy on her. And about Daddy and how he was getting harder and harder to get along with. And disapprovingly about her sister Delia, who was daft about boys and dances and wasn't much help around the house. She asked him if he would like to come down the yard with her while she fed the chickens but refused his gallant offer to carry the bucket of slop for the pigs. "You would only dirty your suit," she said. And all the time her tone was remote and polite, as if she were speaking to Father Coyne himself. He was wishing she'd ask him about the scholasticate, but she never once mentioned it. Not even when they walked back the field to the pond, where she threw some stale bread to the geese and pointed out the one small black gosling in the white flock. "I don't know where he came from," she said. "I call him the priest because he reminds me of you." But she didn't even smile, and she said no more about the gosling or about him. It was as if his present life were beyond her sphere of interest. Coming back into the house and trying to think of something to say, he remembered that there had been talk last year of her taking a job in Dublin, so he mentioned that. "No," she said, "that didn't happen. I'm getting married." It came out suddenly, her back to him as she put turf on the fire. "I don't know if you heard."

He was caught off guard, standing there in the middle of the kitchen floor, blushing, dammit, and having to swallow a couple of times. "So they tell me." Trying to be casual, but feeling that he sounded like a duck quacking.

"Next month," she said, turning to face him. "That's why I'm going to the dressmaker."

The opening was there of course to say what he came to say, but he was in no condition to avail himself of it. "Good luck," was all he could manage. Then, for the first time since he came, she gave him a smile as she walked past him back into her room off the end of the kitchen.

"Are you happy for me?" she shouted from within.

"Is it what you want?" he shouted back. But she didn't answer. He thought she was changing and tried not to imagine her undressing. Then, a minute later, she came back out, still dressed the same, carrying some clothes that she draped over a chair.

"I have to change to go out." She turned her back to him and pulled her arms out of the sleeves of the gansy she was wearing, then slipped a pullover from the chair over her head. He could feel the reddening spread over his face with the struggle: nature looking for a glimpse of flesh and grace demanding aversion of the eyes. Nature overcame, but Catherine got the pullover on and the gansy off without so much as displaying a bare arm.

"You're marrying Thomas Ryan," he said, going over and standing by the fire and trying desperately to sound normal.

"Yes." Nothing more, her back still to him. She took a red skirt from the back of the chair and stepped into it, pulling it on over the black one she was wearing. He could feel the blood pressure rise.

"What made you decide on Thomas?" he croaked.

"You're a fine one to ask a question like that." She swung around, looking him straight in the eye while she bent and pulled the black skirt out from underneath the red. "Now, if you had been available yourself . . ." Her mouth smiled sweetly, briefly, as she picked the black skirt off the floor, folded it, and draped it over the chair.

"Don't you think he's . . ." he started, but then let a shrug say the rest, too embarrassed to continue.

"Old enough to be my father?" She was still staring at him, but the smile was gone. "Well, let me tell you, Father O'Brien, there's many a good tune left in an old fiddle. And the only thing old about Thomas Ryan is his age. He's younger and livelier than a lot of people I know who don't have half his years." And she grabbed the clothes off the chair and swept away into the room.

There was nothing more to be said. "I'll be going now," he mumbled when she came back out. "I don't want to keep you late for your dressmaker."

"Arrah, sit down and have a cup of tea," she said, cheerfully now, smiling a real smile, as if somehow the reserve between them were removed with her old clothes. "The dressmaker can wait. It isn't every day a priest comes to visit me. Especially one that's an old flame." That smile was the Catherine he remembered, roguish and soft. She got two cups and saucers down from the dresser and poured tea from a pot simmering at the fireside. "Sit over at the table now," she said, "and we'll have a good chat about old times."

And they did, though she did most of the talking. She reminisced about their cycling together back to school and the dances they went to in Kilmolara. And about the play that Addis Emmet put on one Christmas in Mulligan's loft that they both had parts in. And about the time, when they were small, that they sneaked into Thomas Ryan's orchard and stole apples from his one good apple tree and got chased by his wicked sheepdog. "Who'd ever have thought," she said in wonder. Still, never a word about how he was doing in the scholasticate. He didn't care to mention it anymore either because the longer they spent talking the more the years were dropping away and he was back again in the days of his youthful lust—yes, he admitted that was what it was— for this redheaded girl he had grown up with. Who was now, God help us, a gorgeous woman and was, God between us and all harm, about to marry that ancient codger, Thomas Ryan, a man they stole apples from when they were both but nippers.

"Did you know that Reddy Ryan is gone on you?" He blurted it at her back when she got up from the table and went over to the fireplace to make more tea. It took a great effort to get the words out because somewhere in the back of his illogical mind he still wanted her all for himself. But he couldn't face Reddy again without having said at least that much on his behalf.

"I had a notion." She said it calmly, taking the kettle off the fire. "The poor lad blushes every time we meet."

"And do you like him?" What came into his mind that he really wanted to say at that minute was, Do you still love *me*. Anyway, he'd have something to tell Reddy.

"Well, I'll tell you, he'd make a great coort." She poured water into the teapot. "We'll let that draw now for a few minutes." She came back to the table. "Reddy is the nicest of the lads, I'd say. And he has great muscles."

"But you wouldn't think of marrying him?" He almost choked on the words. What was wrong with him at all?

"Arrah, don't be daft!" She laughed a high-pitched screech that told him the idea was not so far-fetched. "Sure, the creature doesn't have a penny to his name. Anyway, he'd never have the courage to ask me, he's so shy."

"But if he did, would you?" He had done his duty to Reddy now, and it was tearing him apart inside. He didn't want his Catherine marrying anybody.

"No." She said it quietly, without emotion. "You can't live on love, as they say."

That brought on silence. He drained his cup before he said, "Would you have married me? I didn't have a penny to my name either." He heard the words coming from a great distance, as if he were floating up there somewhere in the sky.

She got up quickly and walked over to the fire again. "The tea should be ready by now." But when she turned with the pot in her hand there were tears in her eyes. And there was hot anger too. "I'd have married you if I had to break stones on the road for the rest of my life," she said fiercely. "But since you've taken yourself out of the running, I'll settle for some comfort instead." She poured tea into his cup until it overflowed on the saucer. "And that's why I'm going to marry Thomas. But you can tell Reddy Ryan from me," she said, looking straight at him and holding the teapot high, "that if he wants a good coort now and again I'll be waiting for him back in Thomas's hay shed."

Phelim put his head down, embarrassed, appalled, his stomach giving warning signals that he might have to run for the outhouse. "You don't mean that, of course. It would—"

"Oh, Phelim! Don't be such a stick-in-the-mud. It was always your biggest failing, I'd say." But when he looked up she was smiling roguishly at him. "Of course I don't mean it. But tell him anyway."

"I'll do no such thing," he said, feeling a bit of relief that she wasn't serious. "It would be a terrible thing to say."

"Go on out of that! There's no harm in it. Tell him."

"I will not!"

"Ah, do! Good lad."

"No!"

"If you don't promise to tell him, I'll tickle you." She laid the teapot down on the table and put her hands on her hips and that look of mischief that he remembered so well came into her eyes. "Remember the way I used to tickle you when you wouldn't do what I wanted?" And the excitement rose in him at the memory of her thin cool fingers squeezing in under his arms and across his chest and down his back and around his stomach. It was the only time they ever used to touch, and the pleasure of it was, sad to say, always matter for confession.

"You can't make me," he said now, knowing he shouldn't say those words because they had always been the invitation for her to start.

"Yes I can." And before he could move she was behind him, her fingers probing his armpits. He tightened his arms and bent his head as he used to do. But the fingers raced up and down his back, and he wriggled and twisted with the unbearable pleasure of it. He had ever been awfully ticklish and would get fighting mad when the lads, or even his sisters, tried to stir him up that way. But Catherine he had always allowed. And he permitted her now. The fingers moved in under his jacket and across his chest and down to his stomach. And then, as they had never done before, they were touching those parts of him that should never be touched, not even by himself except when absolutely necessary, said the moralists. And he just sat there scrunched in a ball, laughing and giggling and chortling and letting her do this thing to him. Finally, when he could take no more, he screamed for her to stop, as he had always done. And she immediately stopped, as she always had. That was their rule.

"You promise now?" Her face red with the passion and her breath coming fast.

"I promise, I promise, I promise," he yelled. That too had been part of the ritual.

"I'll let you off further punishment, then," she said. Always her final statement after a tickling. But when he looked up he saw in her eyes a white fire he had never seen before. He needed to run, the back of his mind said loud and clear, but he couldn't move a muscle. Not even when she leaned over him, still in the chair, and kissed him full and hard on the lips.

If it weren't for her he'd still be there. "Get out of here quick," she yelled, pulling back suddenly, as if she had been burned, "before I get you into serious trouble."

He shambled home, his mind in a terrible fog, reliving, while trying not to, the pleasure of her touch. It was wrong, it was sinful, and going back over it in his mind was sinful. And falling in love with her all over again was worse. Just when he thought he was free and clear of that kind of thing. He had a vow of chastity, for God's sake!

All the rest of the afternoon he brooded and worried and tried to pray. He had been guilty of terribly unpriestly behavior. Maybe it wasn't mortal sin because he had not given it full consent, he thought but wasn't sure, but if they knew about it in the scholasticate he'd surely be asked to leave. Then he thought of what he had to tell Reddy, and he worried some more. She was going to marry Thomas, that was for sure. But at least she said she liked Reddy; that might cheer him up. And she might have married him if he had money; no, he couldn't tell him that. Or that she would surely have married himself, Phelim, if he had stayed around. And he certainly couldn't relay that she thought Reddy a good coort and would be waiting for him in the hay shed. That was a terrible thing to say, and it was a side to Catherine that he had never known before. But he had promised her he'd tell Reddy. Yes, but . . . No buts; he had promised. But it would be wrong. You're not bound to keep a promise to do something that is wrong. He was not going to mention it.

But he did anyway. The woebegone expression on Reddy's face when he informed him back at the head of the boreen that she was definitely going to marry Thomas made him tell him all. First the bit about the money, as if that knowledge would somehow be a consolation for losing her. And when that didn't make things better he mentioned that she had said Reddy would be a good coort. And it was then, without meaning to, he assured himself after, that he blurted out the bit about the hay shed.

"Christ Almighty!" Reddy grabbed his favorite rock off the wall and hurled it farther up the road than he had ever thrown it before. But whether it was the rejection or the invitation that gave him the strength, Phelim couldn't tell.

"You wouldn't want to take that bit too seriously," he said, suddenly worried that his tale-telling might become an occasion of sin for his friend. And immediate sin for himself, responsible for inducing the occasion.

Reddy retrieved the rock and threw it again, though this time not nearly as far. "'Tis you're the lucky lad, O'Brien," he said, replacing the stone on the wall, "to be away from all this stupid bleddy nonsense. Maybe I should become a priest myself. Or at least a Christian Brother." But the combination of pained eyes and crooked grin betrayed a determination that was far removed from the resignation of celibacy.

Phelim was in a panic of blame at himself all night, wondering what Reddy might do. He was still gnawing at the worry when he passed Thomas Ruane and Pat Moloney on his way home from mass the next morning. He made oblique reference to it when he went to confession to Father Coyne on Saturday evening and felt just a little bit better afterwards, arguing that it was probably no longer a sin on his soul. Sunday, the day before he went back to the scholasticate, Creevagh played Ballindine in the O'Hara Cup semifinal. Though they lost by two points in a tough, close match, Phelim was elated coming off the field because he had played a great game, scoring five of Creevagh's total of nine points. Afterwards he looked around for Reddy to talk about the match.

"Is it Ryan you're looking for?" Seamus Laffey asked. Seamus was still changing out of his togs behind a wall. "I think he has better company to go home with this evening." He pointed a finger over the wall to where Reddy and Catherine McGrath were walking out through the gap at the far end of Mulligan's field, heads down and close together as if engaged in intimate conversation.

A month after his return to the scholasticate Phelim had a letter from his mother in which she briefly mentioned the wedding of Catherine McGrath and Thomas Ryan. "Maggie Ruane said the bride didn't look any too happy at the altar," was her only comment. Further on she said, "Thomas told your father the day before the wedding that his godson, Reddy, will be working the land for him from now on, since he's getting too old to do it all by himself. That will be a big help to poor Reddy, the creature; it will put some money in his pocket so he won't have to go off to England like the rest of the lads."

Though it was against the rule, Phelim spent that afternoon recreation period on his knees in the chapel, trying to keep his head from exploding.

The

Pride

of

Turloughmor

"BEGOB, she's a fine cut of a girl." Paddy Moran was watching to see if Eileen Maille would show a bit of leg. She didn't. She got on her bicycle as gracefully as that awkward machine would allow and pedaled away from the church gate with her dress modestly covering her knees.

"Why don't you cycle home with her, Paddy?" Matty O'Brien poked Seamus Laffey with his elbow. "He's panting like a sheepdog every time he sees her."

"Do you think she'd have me?" Paddy straightened his shoulders. A big lump of a lad and a great man with the football. But a bit shy when it came to the ladies.

As indeed were they all. Especially when the lady was

Eileen Maille. They'd watch wistfully for her coming out of last mass on Sunday, hoping she'd notice them. A lovely girl entirely, Matty O'Brien summed up. But divil a one of the three had the spunk to do more than say hello to her.

"Ah, she's a bit old for me," Paddy said, shrugging, by way of explaining his reticence.

"She is not," Matty retorted. "She's an age with yourself. We were all in the same class in Creevagh."

"But she's a bank clerk now and I'm only a bogman."

Seamus Laffey, standing between the two, said nothing. He'd like to tell them to shut their gobs and not be talking about Eileen Maille as if she were a prize heifer. *His* Eileen was how he thought of her. The way he always thought of her, ever since they had stood across the floor from each other in Creevagh National School. He still got goose pimples remembering the way she would look at him with those big, dreamy eyes of hers. Thirteen he was then and in love the way thirteen-year-olds are in love. But he stayed in love, and he was still in love. Though it was the most hopeless kind. What Paddy said was true of himself as well: she was a bank clerk and he was a bogman. Even though they were neighbors. And he had been the best scholar in his class in Creevagh. Better even than Eileen Maille. But he was needed at home on the land and had gone for only one year to the Christian Brothers. And now he hadn't the courage to ask her to dance. Not even once last Sunday night in Kilmolara ballroom.

He was going to ask her tonight, though, God willing, if she was there. He had thought about it and thought about it all week long, when he was stooking oats and weeding beet and milking cows. Especially when he was weeding because that was such a monotonous job. And the thought stayed in his mind all day Sunday. So after he and the brothers finished the milking in the evening he washed his face and hands and slicked his hair with water on the comb and got back into his good suit.

He tiptoed inside the door of the church for Benediction just as the girls' choir started the "Tantum Ergo." Father Coyne might be late starting mass in the morning but he was always on the altar for Benediction at exactly eight o'clock. They said it was because he played cards on Sunday night.

Outside afterwards, with the smell of the incense still in his nostrils, Seamus Laffey congregated with the lads. They talked football and watched the girls leave. Eileen Maille wasn't among them. She hardly ever came to Benediction.

"Where's herself, Paddy?" Matty asked slyly. Paddy blushed a bit, but you could see by his big, dimpled grin that he was pleased.

Seamus Laffey had the butterflies in his stomach. Vexed with Matty for always associating Paddy Moran with his Eileen. Faith, he'd show them tonight. He was going to ask her for a dance. A brave lad now, of course, he recognized. But would he do it when the time came?

The three of them cycled into Kilmolara and hung around outside the Town Hall ballroom. Ostensibly talking, but the real business was spotting form as the girls went in. Seamus looking out for Eileen Maille, knowing Paddy Moran was too. She rode up at about half ten with May Mangan and Mary McHugh, looking like a queen in a gorgeous flared green dress. She smiled at them and said hello. They couldn't wait to follow her inside.

The dance was in full swing. A famous band from Castlebar had the place packed. The lads stood by the wall on the men's side and watched the action. A slow foxtrot and the lights dim and the couples holding tight. Seamus could already feel things happening that might need explaining to Father Coyne at his next confession.

He didn't see her for a while. Too many bodies and not enough light. Then an opening in the crowd let him spot her briefly. Up dancing already. With a townie. A fellow he'd seen before. And didn't like. Red hair and freckles and delicate-looking hands. He had noticed the hands in particular: the kind that never milked a cow or forked hay or weeded turnips. Someone had said he was a bank clerk too. Probably played golf as well.

Anyway, he was shuffling around with Eileen. Almost cheek to cheek. Seamus could feel the jealousy rising up inside him. He didn't want anyone dancing cheek to cheek with his Eileen. Much less this freckled townie.

The music stopped and the lights went up. The men came back to their side of the hall. The women went to theirs. The floor was empty until the band leader announced the next dance: a rumba. Seamus Laffey hated rumbas; he couldn't do them well. Maybe he'd wait out one more dance.

"Now's your chance, Paddy," he heard Matty O'Brien shout above the noise.

By Jasus, he was going to get her before Paddy Moran. Moving the moment the drums were struck. Not able to see her as he crossed the floor, eyes going every which way. Then there she was, coming out of the crowd of women, the red-haired townie holding her hand. Floating right by him, so close her dress rubbed him lightly. Without so much as a notice. Smiling at the fecking freckled bank clerk. He wanted to cry. For God's sake, he hadn't cried since he was ten, but he felt like it at that moment.

Now he couldn't go back or the lads would tease him. He asked the first girl he met. She was nice: soft and warm in his arms and easy to talk to. The kind he'd normally want to dance with again. But not tonight. He hardly noticed what she said or what he said or how badly he danced the rumba. His mind and his eyes were on Eileen Maille dancing with the red-haired townie.

She danced with the prick all night. Paddy Moran scowled till Matty stopped teasing. Then he went off and danced with any girl he could find. Seamus Laffey stood by the wall and brooded and wished he hadn't come.

At three o'clock when the last dance was announced they saw her leave with the townie.

"Isn't that the divil and all," was all Matty O'Brien could say. The other two had nothing to offer.

They cycled home against the wind. Near Creevagh a motorcar came towards them, heading back into Kilmolara, its lights dazzling them for half a mile.

"That's fecking freckled face's car, I bet," Paddy Moran panted. The wind was strong that night.

Saturday evening after milking they met as usual at the head of Turloughmor boreen. By the grace of God and Father Coyne the three of them were members of the Pioneer Total Abstinence Association, which kept them away from drink and the comfort of Gannon's pub in Creevagh. Their favorite perch was the double wall opposite the boreen. It was once the front of old Jack Coleman's shed. Jack was dead now these past ten years, and his little thatched house and shed were just bare wall ruins.

For a while they took turns heaving their favorite rock, a smooth, almost circular chunk of limestone that Matty O'Brien had turned up last spring when he was ploughing. Paddy Moran, as usual, tossed it farthest: twenty-three and a half feet, measured by Matty's size eleven boots and marked with a large pebble as the throw to beat.

"Are we going dancing tomorrow night?" Seamus asked casually.

"Why wouldn't we?" said Paddy, taking one final heave. It fell short of his best throw.

"He wants another crack at Eileen Maille," Matty razzed.

"I'm going to ask her out." Paddy made the announcement from his seat on the wall, solemn as a judge pronouncing sentence.

"Good on you!" Seamus Laffey managed, but it almost choked him to say it.

"You are like hell," Matty jeered. "You're all talk and no action."

"Bet you a half crown," said Paddy.

They gave Seamus Laffey the money to hold. The idea of them betting over his Eileen stuck in his craw, but he said nothing.

Sunday morning after mass Paddy Moran had his bike at the ready. No sooner had Eileen Maille mounted hers than his leg was over the crossbar and he was pedaling out the road after her, his unbuttoned jacket billowing in the wind. They saw him catch up just before they disappeared around a bend. Seamus Laffey went home and could hardly eat his dinner with the pain in his stomach.

In the afternoon they were back in Mulligan's field with the rest of the Creevagh team for a bit of football practice. Afterwards they walked their bicycles down to Gannon's for a mineral.

"Well?" Matty asked outside after he had quenched his thirst with a long swig on the bottle.

"Well what?" said Paddy, playing the innocent.

"Well, what about Eileen Maille?"

"Mister Freckles is picking me up in his fancy motor car and taking me to the dance," Paddy minced in his best falsetto.

"Jasus!" Matty O'Brien almost choked on his drink.

"Well, that beats the fecking band." Seamus Laffey lifted the back of his bike and spun the wheel viciously.

There was silence for a while except for the whirring of the tire. Then Paddy Moran said vehemently, "A few skelps on the backside with a good stick might take care of the blackguard."

"Begob, maybe you should wait for him at the head of the boreen and tell him to bugger off," Matty speculated.

"We could *all* wait for him," Paddy suggested. "With sticks."

"You can't stop her seeing the fecker if she wants to," Seamus Laffey said morosely.

"But we could stop the fecker from seeing her." Matty was the astute one when it came to fine distinctions.

"Well, supposing we're up at the head of the boreen when he comes in his fancy car and we tell him she lives somewhere else. That way he might never find her." This was Seamus Laffey's idea. He was remembering the time last year when Michael Brown had told Garda Kirwin a like kind of fib. There had been an altercation the previous fair day and a fellow had accidentally bounced his head off Michael's swinging blackthorn. Anyway, Seamus and Michael were standing at the top of Turloughmor boreen when the Garda rode up from Kilmolara and asked if they knew where Michael Brown lived.

"Begob I do," said Michael. "If you go on for about two more miles—Irish miles—you'll come to a boreen on the righthand side. If you go down there for about a mile, you'll see a thatched house, and that's where Michael Brown lives." And they sat on the road and roared laughing after the Garda went off to find a boreen that didn't exist.

"We could put stones in the way so he couldn't get by," Paddy Moran suggested.

It was then that Matty O'Brien had his brainstorm. "We could build a wall across the head of the boreen just before he comes." They looked at him, and they looked at each other. Seamus Laffey stopped spinning his wheel and threw his cap into the air.

"Fecking genius," Paddy Moran roared and almost winded Matty with a thump on the back.

"Eileen's mother goes to Benediction," Seamus said. "We'll have to wait till she goes home."

They didn't go to Benediction Sunday evening. Instead, dressed in work clothes, they sat on Jack Coleman's wall and waited. The long evenings were getting shorter; it was almost dark when Matty announced, "Here comes the jockey."

Mrs. Maille came pedaling slowly back the road. She

was a small woman, and the distance between saddle and pedals required a little leg stretching. It was her side-to-side motions that earned her the nickname.

"Aren't ye going dancing?" she shouted as she wobbled in the boreen. She knew their habits.

"Later, ma'am," Paddy Moran shouted back respectfully.

"Let's start then," Seamus Laffey said urgently when she was out of sight. He had his own ideas about this night.

In no more than a half hour, with light from Matty O'Brien's storm lantern and stones from Jack Coleman's shed, they built a wall across the head of the boreen. Then with spades they dug scraws from Jack's yard to match the road bank on either side of it.

"'Twill do," Matty said, surveying their handiwork with the lantern held high. "A fellow coming along in a motorcar couldn't tell the difference."

"He'll be coming soon, I'm thinking," Seamus said.

But it was almost another half hour before the headlights of the townie's car pierced the night sky as he climbed up the far side of Bowgate Hill. They went into the ruin of Jack Coleman's house and waited, crouching. From the top of Bowgate the headlights cast a dim shadow on the road that grew brighter and brighter. The hum of the motor grew louder. Then they heard the crunch of tires on gravel. The car went slowly past.

"We fixed the fecker," Matty O'Brien chortled.

"He'll be back," said Paddy Moran the pessimist. He was. The headlights came towards them again.

"He must have turned in Johnny Lydon's yard," Seamus said. He wanted Freckles to go away. Paddy Moran too. The world of people who would like to take his Eileen from him. He was sure she'd fall for him if he let her know he was keen. Remember the way she'd look at him in school. And how she smiled at him last Sunday night going into the dance.

Freckles cruised by, even slower this time. At one point he stopped, just beyond the walled up boreen. They thought he was going to get out. But then he moved on. They watched the lights go over the Bowgate and vanish into the black night.

"That's it," Matty said, walking out Jack Coleman's doorway.

But it wasn't. The shafts of light rose up from the Bowgate again and the headlights appeared over the top. Ever so slowly they returned. The lads, bent low on the kitchen floor, were sure this time he had discovered their ruse: he stopped right by their new wall for what seemed like hours. Then, crunching gravel, he inched backwards fifty yards and stopped.

"He's suspicious, I'd say," Paddy whispered.

"Psst!" Seamus Laffey was looking cautiously around the doorway. The townie had left his car and was walking along the section of road that was lit by his headlights. He was facing the wall as if searching. Then he turned around and headed across the road towards them.

"Leave him to me," Matty O'Brien whispered fiercely.

A piercing wail shattering the still night. Seamus Laffey was startled by the suddenness of it. Mournful and terrifying, as if screaming grief for every sin that was ever committed since the beginning of time. The sound of a soul being hurled into eternal agony. It came from beside him, and he knew it was only Matty's imitation of the banshee, yet it made the hairs of his nape rise up and the fingers of death ripple chillingly down his spine.

The townie, with no such inside knowledge to counteract this awful eruption of supernatural terror, hesitated only till his initial paralysis subsided. Then, like a sprinter at the sports of Kilmolara, he raced for his motorcar. They heard in quick succession the slam of a door, the protest of tires on stone as the car roared past them, and the fast-receding sound of an overworked engine.

"I don't imagine he'll come back," Matty said complacently. He didn't. They speculated on how he'd get home by alternate route. He'd have to go to Kilsaggart, they decided, and take the road from Kilsaggart to Ballindine till it met up with the Kilmolara road. Then they dismantled the wall.

"'Tis a bit late to go dancing, I suppose," Paddy Moran said nonchalantly when they were done.

"It is," Seamus Laffey agreed, in a hurry to be away. "I'm feeling a bit tired myself." He went back the boreen home, washed his face and hands, combed his hair, and got into his Sunday clothes.

"Isn't it a bit late to go dancing?" His mother was sitting by the fire knitting. His father was snoring in his chair with the newspaper on his lap.

"It's only half ten," he said. "I'll be there by eleven." He cycled down the boreen to the Mailles' house. To see Joe, Eileen's brother, was his excuse. He went to the back door and stepped in after knocking. Joe and the mother and Eileen were in the kitchen, sitting around the fire. Eileen dressed up as if she were ready to go somewhere.

"Bring up a chair," Mrs. Maille said. "It's getting a bit chilly out there."

The

Pride

of

Turloughmor

57

"It is," he agreed.

The conversation languished after that. Mrs. Maille, who usually couldn't stop talking, had nothing to say. Eileen was like a seated statue, staring into the fire. Didn't even look at him after barely saying hello when he walked in. Joe, after a remark about it being likely to rain tomorrow, lapsed into silence. It wasn't like them at all. Seamus Laffey searched his mind for something to talk about, wondering if they knew what he and the lads had done. They were the kind of people who might know and not say anything now. But they'd make you aware of it in their own good time. He said finally, "Would you like to go to the dance?" Talking to Joe, who was in old clothes and wellingtons, looking as if he had just come in from milking.

"I'm a bit tired now," Joe said. "But there's a woman over there who's raring to go and no one to take her." Pointing to his sister.

"Ah," said Seamus Laffey, tongue-tied now that the moment of truth was upon him.

"I don't want to go," Eileen snapped.

"There was a fellow supposed to take her in his motorcar," Joe said, unperturbed, cruel in the way brothers are cruel to sisters. "But he didn't turn up."

"Musha, maybe he'll come yet, with God's help." A kind woman, Mrs. Maille, who believed in the goodness of mankind.

For an instant Seamus Laffey felt shame for what they had done. That was the instant Paddy Moran walked in the door, and he dressed to kill.

"Well, look who's here," Joe said. You could see he was pleased; he and Paddy were friends. But he was

Celibates

&

Other

Lovers

58

puzzled because Paddy Moran hardly ever came to the house. He and Joe's father—God rest him, he died last year—hadn't hit it off too well.

"I thought I'd drop in to see how ye were doing." The sly grin that Paddy brought with him disappeared the moment he spotted Seamus Laffey by the fire.

"I'd say you were going dancing too," Joe said. "There's a fellow here wanted me to take him, but it's hard to do a tango in wellingtons."

"How are you?" Paddy in the middle of the floor, ignoring Seamus, gawking at Eileen.

She scarcely looked at him. "Not too good," she said, and she said no more, just continued staring into the fire. Even Paddy Moran was at a loss for words.

"Would ye like a cup of tea?" Mrs. Maille was a great woman for the tea.

"Ah, no, no thanks." Seamus Laffey was chagrined, his plans for the night destroyed entirely by this unexpected intrusion. He might as well go home. On the other hand, he couldn't walk out and leave the field clear to Paddy Moran. "Come on, Paddy," he said on a sudden impulse. "Let's go to Kilmolara."

"Will you come dancing?" Paddy was still gawking at Eileen, who continued to ignore him.

"I won't," she said without so much as glancing at him.

"Right so." Paddy, crushed but proud, headed for the door. "We'll be seeing you."

As they were walking out, Eileen said, "Maybe I will." She went into a room off the kitchen and was out in a minute with her coat on.

"It's better for you," Mrs. Maille said, "than sitting by the fire waiting for that amadhan in his car."

They cycled to Kilmolara in almost total silence, Eileen between the two lads and not saying a word. Once inside the ballroom she left them and stood with the women. At the next dance Paddy Moran crossed over and asked her out. She danced with him but then went back to the women's side again. It took all Seamus Laffey's courage to walk over and ask her. A slow waltz and her hair in his face and he not able to think of a single thing to say that wouldn't sound totally stupid. And not a word out of her either. Worse, the stiff way she held him said she didn't want to be here at all. He was glad when the music stopped. The townie appeared at that moment. Right in front of them on the crowded floor, as if he had dropped suddenly from the ceiling.

"I tried to find you," he shouted straight away at Eileen over the noise, ignoring Seamus Laffey as if he were no more than a head of cabbage. He seemed a bit short of breath.

"Did you now?" Eileen said tartly. "Well, you didn't make a very good job of it."

"I couldn't find your boreen." The freckled lad was almost wailing.

"He couldn't find the boreen," she mimicked, her eyebrows raised, looking for the first time that night at Seamus Laffey. "Well, we may live in the back of beyond, God help us, but we do have boreens to get in and out of, and they're not too hard to find. You had no trouble with it last Sunday night, if I remember."

"I know where it is," the townie said in real earnest. "And I went there this evening and it wasn't there. I swear to God it wasn't there."

Seamus Laffey was trying hard to keep a straight face.

"Turloughmor boreen disappears!" Eileen waved her hands in the air. "I can see the headlines in the *Irish Independent* tomorrow."

"What's the trouble?" Paddy Moran appeared out of the crowd.

"This joker says he couldn't find Turloughmor boreen tonight," Eileen said. She was laughing, almost hysterically.

"No, really!" The townie was getting excited. "I walked up and down looking for it. I remembered it was right opposite that old ruin of a house. The ruin was there all right, but the boreen wasn't."

"Jasus," Seamus Laffey said dramatically. "I hope it isn't what I think it is."

"And what do you think it is?" The townie looking snootily at him.

"Well," Seamus said mysteriously, "that's the third time I heard of someone not being able to find Turloughmor boreen." He looked hard at the townie. "Was it dark?"

"Of course it was dark. I came—"

"They say back at Gannon's pub," Seamus said, ignoring the dancers swirling around them, "that old Jack Coleman, who lived in the house at the head of the boreen, once tried to court a girl from Turloughmor. But her father turned him away because he wanted her to marry a rich farmer from Ballindine. The story is that Jack used to stand at the head of the boreen after that with his ashplant at the ready and try to stop the Ballindine fellow from going in. Later, they say, he went soft in the head and tried to stop *any* young lad that was going courting in Turloughmor."

"I often heard them talking about that." Paddy Moran nodded sagely.

"Shortly after Jack Coleman died," Seamus Laffey continued, "the Lord have mercy on him, Packy Grimes from Creevagh came up there on his bike one night. He was doing a line with a woman from Turloughmor—who since went to England, but that's another story. Anyway, when he came to Jack Coleman's house he went to turn in the boreen. But, do you know, there was no boreen. On my solemn oath. Packy swore it to everyone in Gannon's pub that night. He went back to Gannon's in an awful hurry after he heard the banshee wailing inside the ruin of Jack Coleman's house." Seamus paused for effect, watching the townie. He had his attention now. "But do you know the sad part?" he said. "Poor Packy Grimes was dead within the week."

"Go on out of that!" Paddy Moran was shocked. "You don't mean it?"

"You might say it was a coincidence," Seamus Laffey said, looking at the dancers and keeping his eyes well away from Eileen Maille, "only the same thing happened to a fellow from Kilsaggart a couple of years later. He was after a girl in Turloughmor too. And he couldn't find the boreen either. And he heard the banshee wail. And he was dead a week later."

"Did you ever hear such superstitious rubbish?" But there was a quaver in the townie's voice.

"And you think that's why Michael couldn't find the boreen tonight?" Eileen Maille asked, and she looking dead serious at Seamus Laffey.

"I'm not saying it is and I'm not saying it isn't," Seamus said. "But he said he couldn't find the boreen. Did you hear the banshee wail?" He put the question to the townie in the kind of hushed voice he remembered Jack Coleman using when telling ghost stories by the fire. Many's the night he had crept home in terror as a nipper after listening to old Jack's tales of devils in graveyards and dead priests in locked-up haunted rooms.

"I have to go now," the townie said. "There's a man waiting for me outside."

"You're a terrible liar entirely, Seamus Laffey," Eileen Maille murmured. They were doing a slow foxtrot and her lips were almost touching his ear.

"How so?" He knew by the way she was holding him that she wasn't too upset.

"How did you make the boreen disappear, anyway?" she asked.

He told her. And he told her why. Only he didn't let on it was Paddy Moran that wanted to ask her out. Instead, amazed at the courage her nearness gave him, he said it was because he wanted to ask her out himself.

"Are you vexed at me?" He couldn't look at her.

"Of course I'm vexed," she said. "I could have been driven here in a car tonight by a respectable gentleman instead of having to cycle in and out with a pair of bogmen." She held him at arm's length with her head back, and there was that soft, dreamy look in her eyes that he remembered from seventh class in Creevagh National School. "But I think I prefer the bogmen."

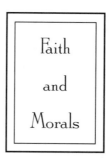

Faith

and

Morals

WHEN Philpot Emmet was only eighteen years of age and Annie May McTigue was nineteen they both ran away from home. Not together, mind you. Philpot was the first to leave, taking the train one Monday morning from Kilmolara to Dublin and hurrying from there to London by train, boat, and train, respectively. Just two days later Annie May followed, in effect the minute she heard of her sweetheart's unexpected departure. You never heard such commotion in the parish of Creevagh. People talking behind their hands to make sure the children couldn't hear. And shaking their heads sadly and muttering phrases like "the blackguard" and "might at least have stayed to face the music." "Bad blood will out" and "a decent man, the creature" were other comments heard, but these referred specifically to Mr. Addis Emmet the schoolmaster, himself a most respectable man indeed but, unfortunately, father of the absconding scoundrel. Father Coyne was confidently expected to raise the matter in the pulpit at first mass on the Sunday after the word was out, but to great general disappointment he never mentioned the unfortunate subject. "If it wasn't Addis Emmet's son he'd have plenty to say," sharp-tongued Maura Higgins remarked to Catherine Ryan the minute they stepped outside the church door after mass was over.

"How so?" Catherine asked, only half her mind on what her friend was saying, the other half being occupied with watching Reddy Ryan talking to Eileen Maille outside the gate.

"You know well that Addis and Father Coyne have always been very great," Maura said. "At least they were before Dr. Browne and his scheme came along." This last was a reference to a proposal by the minister for health of the Irish Republic to provide free health care for mothers and their children. A proposal that smacked of totalitarian Communism, Father Coyne had said from the pulpit a few Sundays before. And of course on this subject as in all else he was in full accord with the cardinal, archbishops, and bishops of Ireland. But not with Mr. Emmet, who told Jack Higgins, county councilor and Maura's husband, that he favored the scheme. "For once in my life I'm in agreement with Addis Emmet," Maura added.

"You're a terrible woman, Maura Higgins," said Catherine. "One of these days they'll excommunicate you." And indeed it was Maura's general practice to contradict established wisdom and established authority and take the side of the underdog in any argument. That practice had landed her in trouble with Father Coyne not too long ago when she said that Communism wasn't really all bad, you know. "What does Jack think about the mother and child?" Catherine was babbling, really; she didn't give a tinker's damn what Jack Higgins thought about anything, but she was desperately trying to ignore Reddy Ryan and Eileen Maille, who were laughing heartily as she passed them.

"My husband," said Maura, "wouldn't give you a straight answer on whether the sun rose this morning." And certainly with regard to the mother and child scheme, the county councilor held a position of evasive neutrality. In stark contrast to his political party, Clann na Talmhan, which was vociferously ambivalent on the subject.

"And I suppose you're in favor of Pisspot and Annie May running away too," said Catherine.

"Well, they showed a lot more spunk than some people I know," Maura said. "Myself included. And it certainly was a better thing than staying around to be forced into a wedding. If you know what I mean."

"You don't think," said Catherine, shocked out of trying to decide what she'd say to Reddy next time she saw him, "that Annie May is . . . Really, Maura, you're terrible."

Maura let out a screech of laughter. "Well, you're the innocent one, Catherine Ryan! Why in God's name do you think the lad left town in such a hurry? And why do you think Jimmy McTigue let his daughter follow him? Of course it's not surprising that it happened. Considering the way Pisspot was mauling the girl in public, it was very unlikely that he would leave any crevice untouched, as it were, in private."

And indeed, young Philpot's behavior in recent months had been nothing short of a scandal to the parish. Annie May and himself seen holding hands walking back the road in broad daylight. Spotted by Matty O'Brien kissing behind a wall just before Philpot togged out for the football match against Kilsaggart. The two of them seen heading into a field of ripening oats by the Kellys on their way home from the bog one evening. The stories multiplied. The rumors spread. Father Coyne was informed. He spoke sternly to the wicked pair. He told Jimmy McTigue to keep his daughter at home, under lock and key if necessary. Those were his very words. Mind you, he said nothing whatever to Addis Emmet. Parish priests and schoolmasters could not afford to fall out with each other, and the relationship between Mr. Emmet and Father Coyne was currently strained by their disagreement over the mother and child scheme. Besides, Philpot had started working in the Bank of Ireland up in Galway, only came home on weekends, and, since he acquired his smelly, noisy motorbike, had stopped listening to his father on any subject whatever.

When Phelim O'Brien came down for his summer holidays that year he couldn't help but hear of the scandal. Indeed, he saw it with his very own eyes just a few days after he arrived. Cycling back to confession on Saturday evening, he heard the roar of an engine coming towards him, an unusual sound in the parish of Creevagh in those days. He was standing on the pedals at the time, forcing his way up steep Bowgate Hill. When he got near the top the noise stopped, and then at the bottom of the hill on the far side he saw the motorbike up against the bank of the road. At the same time off to the left he spotted the pair heading for a haycock. Philpot and Annie May, of course. He had already heard about their carrying on, his mother having mentioned the matter discreetly in a letter and his brother Matty sniggering at table just last night over their latest reported exploit.

Now, Phelim at that minute was on fire with spiritual fervor, having just finished the annual scholasticate pre-holiday retreat. Coming home was regarded as a time of trial and temptation to scholastics' vocations, and they were always fortified by a period of prayer and reflection before being let loose. This year the theme of the retreat had been the scholastic as a leaven in the community. "You can be a great example to everyone," Father Dineen said, "just by the way you comport yourself. You don't have to preach, mind you: you are not yet the parish priest, although there may be an occasion when a discreet word from you will turn a friend or relation towards God or away from sin."

And this was just such an occasion, Phelim reflected vigorously, leaping off his bike and clearing the wall and setting off at a fast gallop after the pair. He would tell them, he decided decisively as he raced across the meadow, about the evil of sin and the beauty of chastity and the importance of avoiding dangerous occasions. It would be hard to say this sort of thing to lads of his own age like Seamus Laffey or Paddy Moran, but since he was many years older than Pisspot he was going to be very forthright in his language. He had already selected "If thy right eye scandalize thee" as his scriptural reference when he rounded the haycock and came upon the pair, flagrante delicto, bodies pressed together, arms locked, and kissing so desperately you would think they were trying to suck the insides out of each other.

"Shite!" Pisspot yelled, retrieving his tongue from inside Annie May's mouth and leaping backwards.

"Jesus, Mary, and Joseph," Annie May prayed after she turned and spotted Phelim. "What are you doing here?"

"Christ! I thought you were Father Coyne for a minute," Pisspot said, at first gasping in great breaths but recovering his composure rapidly. Then he flashed that famous grin of his that could charm Attila the Hun and that was in fact known to disarm everybody in the vicinity of Creevagh except his own father and the parish priest.

"If—" Phelim began, but that was all the scripture he could get out of his mouth at that moment.

"So! To what do we owe the pleasure of your company?" Pisspot cut in courteously. Annie May was straightening out her dress, which seemed to have become a bit rumpled in the preceding entanglement. "Mind you, 'tis nice to see you anytime, Phelim. I was saying to Annie May just before you appeared around the haycock that we hadn't seen hide nor hair of you since you came home. Speak of the devil and he'll appear, I always say. We knew you had arrived, of course. Everybody knows when Phelim O'Brien comes home. You're an important man in the parish, you know. And you'll be ordained soon, I expect. And then we'll have to call you Father O'Brien, I suppose."

"What were you doing?" Phelim went straight to the heart of the matter.

"A good question, Phelim. A good question." Pisspot cleared his throat. "My father always said you were the smartest boy he ever had in Creevagh National School. Although there is a lad there now in sixth class, Mickey Heskin from Kildun, would give you a run for your money, they say."

"And what business is it of yours what we were doing?" Annie May asked belligerently. She had stopped fluffing her dress and was staring coldly at Phelim, hands on hips, as if he were a stray cow that had wandered up to the haycock.

"Now, Annie May," said Pisspot, "Phelim is a holy man, and he walks the fields in the cool of the evening meditating on the glory of God and the wonders of his works. Isn't that so, Phelim? And he came upon us just at the very minute I was trying to get that bit of dust out of your eye. You know," he looked all innocence at Phelim, "Annie May and I just came back the road for a spin before going to confession and we were passing by here and we thought we saw smoke coming out of this haycock. 'We better have a look at it,' says I. 'It might be going on fire.' They can do that, as you well know yourself, if the hay is saved before it's dried properly. And sure, we had a bad summer for saving hay this year."

"I don't see any smoke," Phelim said. Talking with Pisspot was like grappling with the eel he and his cousin had caught one summer back on Lough Corrib.

"It must have been just a temporary phenomenon. They do that sometimes, you know. And then when we were slapping at the cock to see where the smoke was coming from, poor Annie May got the dust in her eyes." Pisspot's own eyes were wide with transparent frankness.

There was nothing else that Phelim could say, especially with Annie May standing there looking daggers at him. "I'll be seeing you," he said and turned his back on them. And he resolved as he climbed the wall out onto the road that he would have a long talk in private with Pisspot the first chance he got.

That opportunity presented itself early the following week. He had cycled into Kilmolara to visit an old school friend from his Christian Brothers days who was now a student at Maynooth and was home on holidays like himself. And he was just heading out of town at about eight o'clock with the intention of getting home before dark since he had no flashlamp on his bike when Philpot came roaring into Main Street on his smelly motorcycle. He slowed down and stopped when he saw Phelim.

"Well, if it isn't Father O'Brien himself." Removing his goggles and wiping the corners of both eyes with his index fingers.

"I thought you were in Galway," Phelim shouted over the roar of the engine.

"I came down to see a man about a dog." Pisspot smiled roguishly.

"I'd like to talk with you," Phelim shouted.

Philpot looked wary for a second, then grinned. "I'd be honored, Father," he said, "to be seen talking with a man like yourself. Come on up to Graney's and I'll stand you a drink and we can chat till the cows come home." And without giving Phelim a chance to refuse he revved up the bike and roared slowly up Main Street. Phelim followed. They turned into Glebe, and Philpot stopped outside Graney's public house. He turned off the engine and kicked the stand into place. Phelim stood his bike against the curb.

"I don't think . . ." he began, but Philpot was already heading in the door. There were several men standing at the bar. They looked curiously at Phelim in his black suit and Roman collar.

"We'll sit in the snug, Father," Philpot whispered loudly, winking at the men. "There's more privacy that way."

Phelim was mortally embarrassed. He had been briefly in Gannon's and Mulligan's pubs in Creevagh on occasion, but never to drink. And never had he been inside a snug. If Father Dineen saw him now, he'd likely ask him not to come back to Kimmage.

"What'll it be, gentlemen?" The barman slid back the grill.

"Two pints," said Pisspot. "You'll have a pint, Father, won't you?"

"No, no!" Phelim was nearing a state of panic. "Just a lemonade, thank you."

"A lemonade for the priest, then, and a pint for myself." Pisspot winked at the barman. "We don't want to be getting the clergy drunk, now, do we? Who else can stand up in the pulpit and tell us to be sober and sin not?" When the grill closed he leaned back and looked speculatively at Phelim. "Are you going to give me a sermon?" He put his hand up to stop Phelim from responding. "It's all right if you do. We all need to be preached at now and again. Some more than others, I'd say. And I probably need a good talking to."

"There's a lot of talk about you and Annie May," Phelim said.

"There is, I suppose. But I don't know why, to tell you the God's honest truth. We're only two normal human beings doing what God intended us to do. I saw a picture called *Annie Get Your Gun* up in Galway last week. There's a song in it about a-doin' what comes naturally, and it struck me that that's all Annie May and myself are doing."

"What you're doing is giving scandal," Phelim said firmly.

"Ah, sure, a bit of kissing and cuddling never did anyone any harm." Philpot opened his arms wide. "Maybe the clergy would be better off if they tried it themselves instead of telling people it's wrong." Phelim could feel the anger growing inside him. The grill slid open and a pint of Guinness and a glass of lemonade were handed in. "Here's to a good squeeze!" Philpot grabbed the Guinness and raised it aloft.

Phelim left his drink untouched. "You're giving scandal to the parish," he said.

Philpot's eyes expressed pain and puzzlement. "You can't be serious, Father!" He put down the pint and leaned towards Phelim. "Is it me? A lad who wouldn't knowingly hurt a fly? That's a terrible serious charge, you know. If thy right hand scandalize thee, cut it off and cast it from thee. That's what the Gospel says, isn't it? So what part of me do I have to cut off, do you think?"

Phelim clutched his lemonade for support against the terrible embarrassment that rolled over him. Why did people always make jokes of such serious matters?

"I think," said Philpot after taking a long, slow swig of his pint, "that it's time the people of this parish, and indeed the people of this country, realized that Queen

Victoria is dead. Take the mother and child scheme, for instance. Here's a plan to improve the health of women and children. Now, what could be more laudable, any thinking reasonable man would say, than to make the women and children of this country healthier? And yet I talked to men in Gannon's pub who said it was a Communist plot to take over the people and land of Ireland. And I heard our very own esteemed parish priest condemn the plan from the pulpit of Creevagh church for the very same reason. And I read in the *Irish Times* the denunciation of the plan by the bishops of Ireland. So I ask myself, Am I the only amadhan around who can't see those slimy Communists creeping into Creevagh under cover of this scheme of Dr. Browne's? But then I ask myself, What would those Russians want to come to Creevagh for anyway? Do you know what I mean? I mean, Creevagh is not the back of beyond; it's forty miles west of the back of beyond. It's not as if—"

"Communism," Phelim said, his voice at full throttle to drown the fetid atheistic propaganda emanating from Pisspot's mouth, "is Antichrist! And it is as cunning as Satan himself. It can deceive the ignorant and fool the unwary. It can—"

"Begob, Phelim, you can preach as well as Father Coyne himself. And not too far behind even Michael, bishop of Galway, I'd say. I heard the man give a sermon a couple of weeks ago up in his cathedral." Philpot took a long swig of Guinness. "That's great stuff. You should try it sometime."

"The mother and child scheme," said Phelim, with great vehemence, "is an instrument of totalitarian aggression."

"You don't say!" Philpot raised his glass again. "And is that contagious, Father?" He grinned quickly. "I was only codding. But seriously, I don't understand how making women and children healthy can be a Communist plot."

"Ah, yes!" Only a couple of weeks ago Phelim had rebutted the dangerous equivocation of a scholastic confrere on this very subject. "The absence of a means test to confine the scheme to the truly indigent takes away from the father his Christian role as the primary guardian of his family's health. And we know that the aim of Communism is to destroy the Christian family, that being the short cut to foisting their atheistic propaganda on the world."

"Well, who would ever have thought . . ." Philpot finished his pint. "I think I'll have another one to help me reflect on what you just said." He tapped the grill. It opened. "Fill her up again, Paddy." A hand took away his glass. "So you're telling me that the mothers and children of this country should die like good Christians from bad health so that their husbands and fathers can keep . . . What is it you said that they must keep?"

"The father is the primary guardian of his family's health," Phelim said stiffly. "But that wasn't what we came here to talk about." Veteran that he was now of many a scholastic discussion, he knew a red herring when he heard one.

"But it's important," Philpot said. "It's important. There's a fellow I work with in the bank who says—and I'm not saying I agree with him, mind you—but he says that the country is being ruined by the clergy interfering in matters that are of no concern to them."

"The clergy have a right to speak out on all matters that concern faith and morals."

"They have. They have indeed." Philpot was lowering his second pint at a great rate. "But will you tell me this, Father: What has preventing a child from getting TB to do with faith and morals? There are those who say—and again I'm not saying I agree with them—but they say that whenever the bishops want to stick their noses into anything they have only to proclaim that it's a matter of faith and morals and we're all supposed to bow our heads and shut up."

"We didn't come to talk about the bishops," Phelim said, "but about the carry on of yourself and Annie May."

"Did you ever kiss a girl?" Philpot finished his pint and tapped on the grill again. "I'll have a whiskey this time, Paddy. It's one of the great pleasures in life, you know. You should try it sometime."

"Did you know," said Phelim, feeling it was time to bring his theological wisdom into play, "that the slightest tittle of carnal pleasure deliberately enjoyed outside of marriage is a mortal sin and could result in your being cast into hell for all eternity?" He stared hard at Philpot, the way Father Dineen had stared down from the rostrum at the scholastics while discoursing on this self-same subject during the recent retreat.

"Begob, that's a mouthful, Father." Philpot stopped the glass halfway to his lips. "I heard those sentiments before, mind you—five years with the Cistercians and you hear everything at least twice—but I always had trouble understanding them." He sipped the whiskey. "The trouble for me is the tittle. 'Tis easy to know when you're having a lot of fun, but it's the divil and all to spot a tittle. It comes and it goes so fast, you see. You only know it was there after it's gone, and then it's too late to do anything about it. You don't have the time to savor it, as it were. Take kissing, for instance. Many's the time I've lain awake at night trying to analyze what is it about a woman's lips that gives you the jolt. Sometimes a tittle and sometimes a lot. But it's hard to put your finger, as it were, on the source of the pleasure."

"You're making fun of me now," Phelim said. He sipped his lemonade, feeling the anger rising inside him again.

"Honest to the good God, I'm not!" Philpot's brown orbs were wide with innocent shock. "It's just that I've been thinking about that for years and never been able to understand it. And while we're on the subject, here's another thing that bothers me: I have a terrible time believing that Almighty God is standing up there on a cloud watching and waiting for me to do something out of turn and then jumping up and down and yelling at St. Peter: 'Got him! Emmet got a tittle! Don't let him in.' Do you know what I mean?"

"You're close to blasphemy now." Phelim was shaking with the anger. "I think I'd better go home."

"I hope I didn't upset you, now," were the last words he heard on his way out the door. Only a week later the scandal of the pair's elopement was the talk of the parish.

Phelim couldn't help brooding for the rest of the month that if he had only been a little more patient in the face of Philpot's flippancy the tragedy might never have occurred. But the bitter lesson of failure would make him a better priest, he resolved on his way back to Kimmage. Two weeks later, in a distraction during morning meditation, he did a little bit of calculation in rudimentary biology and realized that the seeds of the scandal had been sown, as it were, some time before his arrival home on holidays. That made him feel better about the entire incident.

Celibates

&

Other

Lovers

The
Coroner's
Inquest

I T RAINED the day they buried Reddy Ryan. A steady
downpour that had no wind behind it, a sure sign it
had no intention of letting up. Water dripped from
the hats and caps and headscarves of the mourners, leaving puddles all over the seats and floor of Creevagh
church. It was a big funeral: Reddy Ryan was a great
footballer and a young man everybody liked, and the circumstances of his death were tragic indeed.

"The angels are weeping for him," Jack Higgins remarked coming out of the church. But in the kind of tone
that suggested he might have his own interpretation for
this piece of old wisdom. "He was a decent young man,"
he added.

79

"He was indeed." Thomas Ryan, leaning on his stick, tipped his bowler hat with his spare hand out of respect for his deceased godson. The wives, Catherine Ryan and Maura Higgins, said nothing. They all stood by the church gate watching the procession, led by Father Coyne and his six mass-servers and followed immediately by Reddy's family, fall into line and move down the street behind Mike Carney's hearse. The Creevagh football team went next, with Seamus Laffey out in front carrying the ball and Paddy Moran holding aloft the team's flag. Then came the long, straggling stream of friends and neighbors, intermingled with those whom Paddy Gannon called the professional mourners, parishioners for whom going to funerals was as important as going to Sunday mass.

It was a short journey from church to tomb. At Gannon's end of Creevagh village, just a few hundred yards beyond the new parish hall and set well back from the Kilmolara road, the graveyard surrounded the ruins of an old Protestant church. A quirk of history, Addis Emmet, the schoolmaster, used to tell his scholars, that restored a little justice to the poor persecuted Catholics of bygone times. Inside the rusty iron gates the path was potholed and muddy and the graves were overgrown with tall grass. The place was a disgrace to the parish, Catherine Ryan was thinking, the tears coming at the thought that Reddy's body was going to lie here until the day of Judgment. She and Thomas stopped well back, out of sight of Reddy's family, while Jack Higgins, county councilor that he was, moved forward to be seen. Maura Higgins stayed behind with Catherine.

Father Coyne read the prayers over the grave while a

mass-server held a big black umbrella over him. "Absolve, we beseech Thee, O Lord, the soul of Thy servant, Thomas Redmond, from every bond of sin, that in the glory of the resurrection he may rise to a new and better life with the saints and elect." Catherine Ryan sobbed, though she tried hard not to. Was his soul in heaven today? And if it wasn't, was it *her* fault? He went to confession last Saturday for the men's sodality. To a curate in Kilmolara so Father Coyne wouldn't know, but still it was confession. But then she and he did what they did on Sunday afternoon in her husband's hay shed. And he was killed on Wednesday morning. So his only hope of salvation was if he made a good act of contrition in between.

"May his soul and the souls of all the faithful departed through the mercy of God rest in peace." Father Coyne closed his book and removed his purple stole and looked around at the assembly. "Dr. Daly, the coroner, asked me to inform you," he said quietly, "that because of the way poor Reddy died there will be a brief inquest immediately in the parish hall. He asks that as many as possible of you attend."

"I'm sorry for your trouble, ma'am," Francie Madden mumbled, sidling up to Catherine as she and Maura picked their way out through the potholes. Then he walked quickly ahead to catch up with some of the lads. Jeering or condoling, you couldn't tell with Francie. But he and Reddy had been thick as thieves, so maybe he knew.

"It's a terrible tragedy," Maura Higgins said for the umpteenth time. She was the only living soul Catherine had ever told about her and Reddy.

"If he was alive this minute I'd run away to England with him. I swear to God I would."

"We all make our mistakes," said Maura, and while there was sympathy in her voice, there was a bit of judgment too.

"I was daft to marry the old codger, wasn't I?" That foolish act was weighing heavily on Catherine's mind since Wednesday. Her own fault, of course. And Daddy's, God blast him. God forgive her. God rest the Dad's scheming soul. He never thought of anything but land and money. Making her marry an old man like Thomas Ryan so she'd have his place when he died. Which would be soon, he promised. But it was five years this month. And Daddy himself had died two years ago. And now Reddy. And the old bastard was still alive.

"You were, girl," Maura said bleakly.

"We could both be in London now and he'd never have been hit by the bloody tractor." She had thought a lot about being in London these past few months. Strangely, though, it was Phelim O'Brien she was always with in her daydreams, not poor Reddy.

"Maybe. But when your time comes they say you have to go anyway. He could have been hit by a bus instead."

"I don't believe in that at all," Catherine said vehemently. "I believe you make your own luck in this world."

"Well, tell me this, then," said Maura. "Do you think it was an accident with the tractor?"

"I don't know." The tears were back in Catherine's eyes. "We'll never know, will we?"

The new parish hall, the pride of Father Coyne and Addis Emmet, looked bleak inside without the colorful

streamers that had been up for the Christmas play. The
mourners took folding chairs from the stack against the
back wall and made uneven rows in front of the table
near the stage where Dr. Daly had spread out some papers. The doctor sat patiently until the scraping of chairs
and the buzz of conversation stopped. Then he stood. He
was a big man, as tall as Reddy Ryan and a lot heavier.
Older, of course, too: the hair was already gone gray on
him, though he still had great black eyebrows that
moved up and down when he talked. "Whenever death
does not come in the natural way," he said in a voice as
smooth as Father Coyne's describing the state of grace,
"as by disease, the law requires that an inquest be held
to determine the circumstances and the cause. To allevi-
ate, as it were, any suspicions anyone might ever have
that skullduggery could have taken place." Something
close to a smile hovered around his face for just a split
second. Which caused some annoyance to Catherine
Ryan, who felt the world should never smile again since
the love of her life was dead. Though there was a confusion in her image of that love: Was it Reddy Ryan or
Phelim O'Brien? "In this case," the coroner continued,
"a young man, Thomas Redmond Ryan, known to us all
as Reddy, was run over by a tractor driven by Thomas
Ryan, his godfather. Now, I personally have known
Thomas Ryan for many years, and I know the kind of
man he is, and I know he would never intentionally hurt
any living creature. But we must observe the formali-
ties."

Fat lot you know about the old codger if that's what
you think, was what was going through Catherine
Ryan's mind as she watched the coroner's eyebrows go

up and down. He was looking around the room, slowly, as if he were counting sheep. There was no sound except for a couple of nervous coughs. "The first order of business then is to appoint a jury of six men. Their duty will be to hear the evidence and render a verdict." He waved to a group of men standing at the back. "Gentlemen, if you please. Would six of you come up here and I'll swear you in."

Boots scraped on the hard tile floor. A small man in a brown hat and a tan raincoat stepped up to the coroner's table. Martin McGreevy from Kildotia, a farmer of few words but a great friend of Thomas Ryan. Five others followed, slow, straggling, bashful men, discomfort in their very walk: Seamus Moran and Packey Dunne and Mick Grady and Wattie Feerick and James Coneely. To a man they were all friends of Thomas. "That's great now," the coroner said. "If you don't mind I'll take your names first."

Oh, God! Catherine felt the tears well up again. She missed him something fierce.

"Now, if you'll raise your right hands I'll swear you in." Dr. Daly raised his own but then quickly dropped it. "I don't suppose any one of you is a relation of the deceased or of Thomas Ryan, by any chance?"

Mick Grady was a cousin of Thomas on his mother's side. He raised his hand. The doctor looked unhappy. He said, "Ah, yes. Well, that being so, we'll have to excuse you."

Mick looked at him as if he didn't know what that meant. "You can sit back there with the rest," the coroner said, and Catherine could see he was a bit annoyed. He looked around again. "I'll need one more, please, then."

"Is it all right for a woman?"

Maura Higgins! On her feet with her hand up as if she were back in Sister Louis's class. The doctor's eyebrows went down till they almost covered his eyes. He stared at her as if she were some species of disease he had never seen before. "Well!" he said. "I don't know. This is always done by men, you know." Polite but at the same time quite firm.

"But why can't a woman do it?" Maura Higgins stood her ground, her hand still in the air. Catherine Ryan was dying of embarrassment.

There was silence for a while. The coroner waiting for Maura to sit down, hoping she'd take the hint. But she didn't. Finally he said, "Well now, that would be highly unusual."

"Please!" Looking straight at him with those big brown eyes of hers. A gorgeous woman, Maura Higgins, who well knew her effect on men when she looked at them like that.

More silence. The doctor standing by his table, not moving. And not a stir out of Maura either. In the end he said, "Well, all right then. I suppose it's all right." But he looked a bit flustered.

"Right so," said Maura, and she stepped forward and joined the men. For a second Catherine Ryan wanted to laugh: Maura always had that effect on her when they were going to the convent school in Kilmolara.

"If you'll all raise your right hands now, I'll swear you in," the coroner said again. And he had them bring up chairs and sit facing the audience. And he told them what they were expected to do: hear the evidence, the facts of the case, he said, and render their verdict accordingly. In all likelihood accidental death, of course, but that was for them to decide.

"If you're ready, then." He sat in his chair, leaning forward, elbows on the table. "I'll first call on Thomas Ryan to tell us exactly what happened."

Catherine Ryan clutched her handbag tightly. Her husband stood, facing coroner and jury, and took off his hat. "I'd like," he said, and then he stopped to clear his throat. "I'd like to begin by saying that I am today the saddest and sorriest man in all of County Mayo over what happened on Wednesday morning. The memory of it will haunt me for the rest of my few remaining days. I was thinking as I stood by the grave just now that it would have been a better thing if Almighty God had taken me, old man that I am, and left the young fellow who was just on the threshold of his life."

Amen, said Catherine Ryan to herself. The old hypocrite. Did he know about her and Reddy? They were always so careful. But if Jack Higgins and Francie Madden guessed, God alone knew who else might have. And if Thomas did . . . On the other hand he never gave the slightest hint. And he was always very friendly with Reddy.

"But God's ways are mysterious," Thomas Ryan continued sagely, "and it's not for us to question. Let me tell you what happened." He cleared his throat again. "As you all know, I bought a tractor a year ago and I've been working with it every day since. So I'm a good driver. Reddy was too, the Lord have mercy on him. Well, on Wednesday morning at about nine o'clock I took a load of hay down to the cattle in the corner meadow, which is about a half mile from the house. Reddy was riding in the trailer with the hay. It was a wet morning, like today, and poor Reddy had on his oilskin cape. He was very fond of the oilskin for the wet day. Anyway, when we got there he jumped out and opened the gate and I pulled in a little ways and stopped and Reddy came up and un-hooked the trailer. 'You can go back now if you like,' he said. 'I'll take care of the rest.' A terribly reliable fellow, Reddy; you could always count on him to do what needed to be done."

Catherine wanted to tell him to stop rubbing his wet hat brim with his sleeve. And not to remind her of Reddy's oilskin. There was a terrible tension inside her, making her want to scream and to run, away from here and away from him. She was left with the wrong Thomas Ryan, was what was desolating her.

"So I put the tractor in forward gear, as I thought, in-tending to swing around and out through the gate. Instead . . ." His voice was shaking. He stopped, scrunching the hat brim tight with both hands till the water dripped from it. The doctor was nodding encour-agement at him. "Instead," he continued, talking quickly now, as if in a hurry to get it over with, "the tractor sud-denly backed up and I felt the jar of it hitting the trailer. But even then I had no notion of what had happened. I got the gears right and moved forward a bit and then got down as quick as I could to see the damage, saying, I re-member, as I did, 'I made a horse's collar of it this time, Reddy.' It was only when I came around to the back of the tractor that I saw him lying there on the ground in front of the trailer."

His whole body was shaking now like that of a man with the ague. He put his hat back on and sat abruptly.

The silence was awful. The coroner was leaning forward, saying nothing till the shaking subsided, like a mother waiting for a child to stop crying. Then he asked, in a very gentle voice, "Do you have any idea, Thomas, how he was hit? For instance, did you get any notion from the way he was lying where the tractor might have run into him?"

Thomas sat there for a minute with his head down, not saying anything. Catherine looked at him, thinking maybe he was having a stroke. Then slowly he got back on his feet. "I did," he said, and his voice was steady. "He was lying in a kind of a lump, with his head under him. I'd say he had his back to the tractor and it smashed him against the trailer."

"Thank you very much, Thomas," Dr. Daly said. "I know this has been a great ordeal for you." He looked around the hall as if he were counting sheep again. "Was anyone else present at the time? Did anyone witness the accident?" There was a long silence. "In that case, then, I'll tell you what my findings were from examining the body." He stood and read from a sheet of paper. "The cause of death was a broken neck. There were bruises on the lower back and the top of the skull that are consistent with the deceased having been struck from behind and the top of his head ramming into the trailer. This would account for all of the injuries, including the broken neck." He shuffled the papers a bit. Then he looked up very solemnly and said, "Does anyone have anything else to say on this matter before we ask the jury to deliberate their verdict?"

Maura Higgins put her hand up. "I'd like to ask one question," she said. "Were Thomas Ryan and Reddy Ryan known to be on good terms with each other?"

There was silence for just a few seconds. Then a voice from the back shouted, "They were not." Great commotion and much scraping of chairs ensued as people turned to see the shouter. "I have something to say about that too." The man's voice was strong and harsh: the sound of a great anger that was trying to get out. Catherine Ryan didn't need to look around because she knew who it was.

The doctor put on his bedside look. "Ah yes, indeed, Mr. Ryan. We all extend our deepest sympathy to you and your family in this hour of sorrow. It is a great cross to bear." And he paused for a moment in reverence. "Indeed it is," he said. Then, seeming at a loss for further words, he waved his arm like the ringmaster of Duffy's Circus. "Please go ahead and speak, Mr. Ryan."

"I'm here to tell you that the death of my son was no accident," Gerard Ryan said, with an edge on his voice that would slice a turnip. You could have heard a pin drop. The coroner was looking a bit confused. The eyebrows bobbed up and down like a cock's comb at feeding time. Catherine Ryan felt she was in the middle of a nightmare. "That slimy shite sitting up there slaughtered my son," Gerard Ryan shouted.

Catherine wanted to die. Oh God! Everything was going to come out now. It was the beginning of hell for her sins.

The coroner found the right tone for the occasion. "Ah yes, Mr. Ryan. It was a terrible thing that happened. Indeed it was. We're all agreed on that. But we all know too that Mr. Ryan—Mr. Thomas Ryan here—would never deliberately harm your son."

"Thomas Ryan had it in for Reddy for a long time,

and he murdered him on Wednesday morning." The father's tone was as hard as the stone walls of Creevagh. "Pay no heed to what the old bugger says. The man's a bloody hypocrite. He always was. And now he's a murderer as well. And he'll rot in hell for killing my son. And I'm here today to see that he swings at the end of a rope for it too."

Dr. Daly's eyebrows were fixed in the up position, as high as they could go. "Do you really believe," he said in a tone of absolute incredulity, "that a man like Thomas Ryan would be capable of murder? And why would he want to murder your son, even if he *was* capable?"

There wasn't a sound from the assembly, yet their silence shouted at Catherine that they all knew why. "He murdered my boy," Gerard Ryan bellowed.

Dr. Daly's eyebrows shot down. His lips puckered in shocked disbelief. "Murder is a terrible charge to bring against a man, Mr. Ryan. Do you have any evidence for it? Anything to prove that Thomas Ryan murdered your son? Were you there in the field when the accident occurred?"

"Faith, if I was it isn't Reddy who would have died, I can tell you that. But I know he murdered him all the same. Thomas Ryan had reason, or at least he thought he had reason, to kill my son. I told Reddy, many's the time. 'Don't turn your back on slimy Thomas,' I said, 'or go near him or work for him.' But he wouldn't listen. If he had he'd be alive today. And this man here wouldn't have murder on his soul. For which he'll burn in hell for all eternity. And hang—"

"Hold it, hold it!" The coroner was waving both arms like a man trying to pen sheep in a corner of a field. "You said that Thomas Ryan believed he had a reason to kill your son. Now, would you mind telling us what that reason was?"

Catherine wanted the floor to open up and swallow her. But Gerard said only, "The reasons are private; they're not something you'd want to discuss in front of people. But they were there. At least Thomas Ryan thought they were there. I myself don't believe they were. But it's what a man thinks that makes him do things."

The coroner leaned back in his chair and folded his arms. "Mr. Ryan, apart from your belief that Mr.—that *Thomas* Ryan had some kind of reason for killing your son, do you have any evidence that indeed he did intend to kill him? Anything at all that might suggest to these gentlemen—and lady—of the jury that this might not have been an accidental death?"

"I am as certain," Gerard Ryan was shouting again, "as I am standing here this minute that he meant to kill him."

The coroner spent a long time looking down at his papers, his mouth puckered as if he were trying to whistle. Catherine could feel the pain coming on in her stomach, like it came in bed when Thomas would say it was time to do their duty again.

"Mr. Ryan," the doctor said, speaking very slowly, as if he were testing each word for size and weight, "I, and everybody here I'm sure, have enormous sympathy for you and your family. It is a terrible tragedy that has taken place. And on such occasions it is only natural to look for a cause. It makes us feel a little bit better if we can put the blame on somebody. Now we know, and Mr. Thomas Ryan acknowledges with great sorrow, that he was the cause of your son's death. But," the doctor's voice was suddenly loud and harsh, "to say that he did it deliberately and maliciously is a very serious charge indeed and not to be made unless you have evidence to back it up." He stared down the hall at Gerard Ryan the way Sister Louis used to glare at a girl who hadn't done her Latin translation.

"I'll tell you so then what they were saying," Gerard Ryan shouted, just as loud as the doctor. Catherine began to shiver. "They were saying that my son Reddy and Thomas Ryan's wife, Catherine, were terrible good friends for people who weren't married to each other."

Catherine was having trouble breathing. Gerard went on relentlessly. "Thomas Ryan knew people were saying this. He knew that his wife and my son were friends from the time they were nippers. And even though there was nothing going on between them that was wrong, people always like to believe the worst and to say the worst. And Thomas Ryan knew what they were saying, and believed what they were saying and he hated my Reddy, and when he got the chance he murdered him."

A lot of chairs were scraped and a lot of throats suddenly needed clearing. Catherine Ryan's head was bent so much that the back of her neck was hurting. She felt, rather than saw, her husband rise beside her.

"I will not have my wife slandered like this," Thomas Ryan shouted. "She is the best and the most faithful wife any man could ever have. And I will not have my deceased godson slandered either. Reddy *was* my godson, you know. A great lad. A great lad entirely." His voice broke and he stopped. Catherine too lost control: desperate heaving, choking sobs, all the more wrenching for her attempts to suppress them. "I heard the rumors," Thomas continued, calming himself. "No man who wasn't stone deaf and three months dead could fail to hear the gossip that goes on in this parish. But I knew it was only old biddy talk. The black envy of people for an old man who had the great good fortune to marry a beautiful young girl. Certainly I heard the talk. But I never believed it. Not for one solitary second." He was about to sit, but then he straightened up again. "One time I asked Reddy about it. 'Reddy,' I said, 'what do you think of those rumors about you and the missus?' And do you know what he said? 'It's a pack of lies,' he said. 'You can't pay attention to what people say. Catherine and me are like brother and sister, and we have been ever since we were in school.' And that was good enough for me; Reddy was always a truthful boy. He'd never tell a lie." His voice cracked again and he paused.

Catherine sobbed convulsively. She had been unfaithful to this good man who believed in her and in Reddy. God forgive her. And for even letting the thought cross her mind that he might have intended poor Reddy's death. She was going to be nice to him for the rest of his days.

"Reddy was like a son to me all his life." Thomas was getting emotional again. "I would have died for the lad. And I wish to God it was me who was killed on Wednesday."

Maura Higgins butted in again. "In fairness to Mr. Gerard Ryan I should tell you that my husband, Jack, told me more than once that Mr. Thomas Ryan didn't like Reddy Ryan, the Lord have mercy on him, at all. He'd say things, Jack said, like, 'He thinks he's clever

but he'll get his one of these days.' Didn't he, Jack?"
Looking over at her husband sitting next to Thomas
Ryan.

Jack Higgins didn't look in the least put out. A great
man on his feet, Jack. It was said he might run for the
Dail at the next election. He stood up and looked
straight at the jury. "'Tis well known," he said, "that a
man should never argue with his wife." He paused. "Especially when she's wrong." He kept a straight face, and
sure enough there were some loud guffaws around the
hall. "But I'll tell you this. I never said any such thing,
and Thomas Ryan never said any such thing in my hearing. Thomas Ryan had great respect for young Reddy,
and he told me so more than once, and he showed it too
in the way he treated him."

Catherine, hunched over and head down, heard the
coroner ask Gerard Ryan if he had anything to add, and
she heard Gerard say, "If he thinks he can get off scot-
free with killing my son he has another think coming."
And she heard the coroner tell the jury to go over and sit
in the far corner of the hall and deliberate their verdict.
But it was all very far away. She felt locked in a box with
no air and she wanted to struggle to get out, but she
couldn't move. There was a buzz of conversation somewhere and the sound of people walking. Then the
coroner's voice burst on her ears again, like sudden
stones falling off a wall. "Ladies and gentlemen, please
be seated; the jury has reached a verdict." More scraping
of chairs and coughing and then silence. Dr. Daly said,
very formally, "Gentlemen of the jury—and lady—what
is your verdict?"

Catherine heard a rough farmer's voice say, "Despite

the opinions of one member, we have no reason to believe that Reddy Ryan's death was not an accident."

"God blast ye all!" The voice of Gerard Ryan preceded the rasp of boots and the slam of the parish hall door.

Thomas's hand clamped tightly on her arm, and he said very quietly, "We'll go home now."

On the Monday after the funeral Catherine Ryan was down the field by the pond feeding the geese. Keeping herself busy to drown the horror of last week. The geese were flocked around trying to pluck the bread from her hands. All except the black gander that stood aloof to the back by himself. "The curse of God on you, Phelim O'Brien," she yelled at the gander. "If you had stayed, none of this would ever have happened." Who needed priests anyway? Black gander in a black suit just to be different from the rest of mankind. Well, next Sunday this black gander was going in the dinner pot; she'd see to that. She spotted Bernie the postman cycling slowly back the road. He stopped by the gate. She threw the remainder of the bread at the geese and headed toward him; it wasn't every day the postman came by.

"God bless the work," he said. A grand man, Bernie. A soldier in the First World War whose life was saved they said by the silver cigarette case he was carrying in his pocket that deflected the bullet intended for his heart.

"You too," she answered.

"I hope it isn't bad news." He foraged in his pouch and pulled out a long, black-bordered envelope. In the kitchen she used a sharp knife to slit it open and straightened out several sheets of folded paper. The first page had large black letters at the top:

ARGEW AND PHIBBS, SOLICITORS

Dear Mrs. Ryan,

We read with great regret in the *Irish Independent* of the death of your husband, Thomas, and hasten to send you our most sincere condolences on this tragic occurrence.

Your late husband was our client for many years, and we would like to assure you at this time that we will be most willing to render you any assistance that is within our purview.

It was your husband's wish that on the occasion of his death we were to forward to you without delay a copy of his last will and testament. We therefore enclose same with this letter.

Sincerely yours,
Morris Phibbs

First she was bewildered. Then she wanted to laugh. Then she wanted to cry. They saw poor Reddy's death in the paper and assumed it was Thomas who had died. But now, should she read the will? It was supposed to be bad luck to read someone's will who wasn't dead. "Being of sound mind . . ." it began. You always had to start your will with that, she had heard somewhere. "I hereby bequeath . . ." Very archaic. "To my wife, Catherine, who has been consistently unfaithful to me, the sum of one penny. And to my nephew, Jack Heneghan of Tobarmor, all lands, property, and money of which I shall die possessed."

The Heirs of Martin Mulligan

ARTIN Mulligan died of a Sunday morning. His death rattle coincided with the ringing of the last bell for first mass. A fitting moment for the poor man to go when he had to go: he used to always leave the house immediately after that bell, running the hundred yards or so to the church with shoelaces untied and shirt only half buttoned and striding up the aisle to the front row on the men's side just as Father Coyne and his six servers were genuflecting before the tabernacle.

Faith, it wasn't going to church that made him rich, they said down at Gannon's pub. They made that remark because in his later years Mulligan went to mass every day. He had a lot to make up for, God blast him, a few bitter ones added. The fellows who drank at Gannon's didn't particularly like Martin Mulligan.

The deceased had his own drinking establishment two hundred yards up the street from Gannon's, on the other side of the church. "Mulligan's Bar, Victuals, and Grocery," the black-and-white sign over his door said. He also had a traveling shop that the oldest boy, Timmy, took around the countryside in the lorry, selling groceries and bags of flour and what have you to farmers' wives and buying up the eggs they had to spare when the hens were laying well. Mulligan bought wool from the farmers too, at shearing time, and took it to Galway by the lorryload to sell. At twice the money he paid them, the same farmers grumbled when they were drinking their pints down at Gannon's.

Martin Mulligan had a finger in every pie. The bar was just a small part of his business, but he had a select, loyal clientele who never, except for Jack Higgins, the county councilor, drank at Gannon's and who rarely said anything derogatory about Martin Mulligan.

At his wake on Monday night, however, the men from Gannon's mingled with the men from Mulligan's, and all drank the health of the deceased from the latter's half barrels. A great wake it was, everyone agreed afterwards. Martin Mulligan was the best-known man in the parish after Father Coyne himself, and everyone who was anyone came to see him off.

They began to come in the afternoon, at first mostly the women. They told Clare, his widow, a big, dark-haired, dry-eyed woman, that they were sorry for her troubles. And they admired the bedroom with the huge featherbed where the remains were laid out in the humble brown of St. Francis. Wallpaper on the walls, my dear, they noted, and horsehair-stuffed chairs, and shiny mahogany furniture: more like a parlor than a place where you'd sleep.

Even some of the children on the way home from school dropped in to see big Martin for the last time. They all knew him well. He would count out the sweets himself whenever they had a penny to buy a few, and sometimes he'd even add an extra one. Particularly for the son or daughter of a man who drank at Gannon's.

It was at night of course that most of the mourners came, especially the men. They arrived on foot and on bicycles, in traps and in sidecars. Even a cart with cribs was hitched to the church rails. Property of Johnny Lydon, who, though (erroneously) said to be even richer than Martin Mulligan, would never buy a fancy sidecar or trap.

Inside, porter and conversation flowed in about equal measure, and Martin Mulligan looking down from above—or up from below, as the case may be—must have been a happy man indeed, surrounded as he was by friends and enemies, supporters and detractors.

"He had a great flair for the money, begob," Pat Moloney told Paddy Gannon. Filling a pint for himself from the half barrel on the kitchen table. Paddy had closed down his own establishment for the evening, out of respect, he said, for the dead. Which caused no little silent shaking of mourning heads because of the known enmity between him and the deceased. But no one suggested he had done so merely because his patrons were likely to have a sudden preference for Mulligan's free porter.

"He could see a shilling was to be made where you or

I would never spot it." Pat took a long, comfortable pull on his pint. "My father told me about the time—it was before the war, and things were bad—Martin found an ass the tinkers left behind on the road. The creature was thin and hungry and spavined, and the hooves were curled on him like a ram's horns. Even the tinkers had no use for him anymore. Begob, Martin pared the hooves and fed the animal for a few months on graveyard grass—they say it's the best. Next time the tinkers came he brushed him down and sold him back to them for a couple of pounds. And sorra one of them lads ever knew it was their own ass he was passing off on them."

"He'd build a nest in your ear and you'd never know it," Thomas Ruane said. "I remember—"

"He wouldn't build a nest in that fellow's ear, I'd say." Paddy Gannon pointed to the Yank Walsh kneeling by the corpse-bed, head down, eyes closed, hands joined on his capacious front. "If you didn't know that man better, you'd say he was praying."

"Faith, 'twould be a sorry day for you when you'd depend on the Yank's prayers, I'm thinking," Jimmy McTigue said.

"The fellow in the bed is beyond praying for now," Paddy Gannon commented in a satisfied kind of way. "God damn the bleddy bastard in hell," he bellowed suddenly. Fortunately the general din muted this unseemly explosion.

The Yank got to his feet slowly, with all the gravity of a man coming out of a conference with the Almighty, opened his eyes, made a quick, wrist-motion wave at blessing himself, and waddled out of the bedroom straight over to Paddy and the porter barrel.

"The Lord have mercy on him," he said to everyone in general. "We won't see his like again."

"A grand man," Paddy Gannon said. "He left some fine porter behind him." He patted the barrel. "Help yourself, Mr. Walsh. Drinks are on the house."

"A decent man." The Yank helped himself. "Him and me go back a long way."

"You do," said Paddy. "I'd say you made a power of money together during the war."

"Divil a bit." The Yank drank long and deep. "There was no money to be made during the war."

"'Tis terrible the way fellows do be skinning lies, then," Thomas Ruane said. "They do it instead of working, I'm thinking. I heard lads swear to me till they were blue in the face that it isn't known what money you and Martin Mulligan made during the war."

"Lies, for sure," the Yank said. He tugged at his collar as if it were too tight. "Sure, this country is a sinkhole of lies. I'll tell you this; if I hadn't come home from America with some money in my pocket I'd be the poorest man in Creevagh today. That's a fact, now. And it was hard work I did to earn that money." He drank some more porter.

"'Tis many a man worked hard and made no money at all," Jimmy McTigue put in.

"Great porter." The Yank filled his mug again. "Martin Mulligan kept only the best."

"I prefer the tea myself," said Pat Moloney. "It's a great comfort, and you never get drunk on it."

"'Tis bad for you," the Yank said. "Bad for your insides. Almost as bad as the coffee. I knew a fellow in New York once who gave up the porter and started drinking coffee. He was dead in a month."

"Scalded, no doubt," Thomas Ruane hazarded. "You have to put a lot of milk in tea. I don't drink coffee myself, but they say—"

"He was run over by a bus," the Yank said.

"I suppose it's because during the war it was so hard to get," Pat Moloney continued, "but I have this awful thirst for the tea in the morning. I can't milk a cow or feed a pig until I've had at least two cups. My mother, God rest her, was the same. When it was scarce she'd use the same tea leaves over and over again. She couldn't afford only the half ounce you'd get with the ration card."

"There were fellows got rich on the tea when it was rationed," Paddy Gannon put in. "Like himself up in the bed." But he was watching Eileen Maille just inside the parlor door talking with Timmy Mulligan. He'd have to speak to her mother about that.

"Ah, sure, the creature didn't make anything from it," the Yank said. "I heard him tell he paid as much for it as he got. He only did it as a favor to the customers. It was the black market fellows in Dublin were making the money."

"And the fellows that brought it down from Dublin," Jimmy McTigue added. "Don't forget them lads."

"Real mystery men they were, those jokers," said Pat Moloney. "No one ever saw them coming, and no one saw them going. Only the tea and the sugar and the cigarettes would suddenly appear under the counter in Martin Mulligan's shop."

"I met a strange fellow once of a fair day in Kilmolara," Thomas Ruane put in. "I said to myself—"

"You used to go a lot to Dublin yourself, Mr. Walsh, in those days." Paddy Gannon was still looking over the

Yank's shoulder at Eileen Maille. A grand girl entirely. "Did you ever see any of those jokers in your travels?"

Eileen Maille wasn't really enjoying her conversation with Timmy Mulligan. She was trying her level best, God knows, but it was hard to get fond of Timmy. It wasn't that there was anything terribly wrong with the boy. He had a bit of polish even, which most of the local lads were sadly lacking. He'd gotten it of course from five years of boarding school with the Cistercians. And he was actually not half bad-looking if you overlooked the infamous Mulligan nose that in profile was a bit like the left side of Croagh Patrick—the view that you'd get of the mountain from Clew Bay.

She was only half listening as she tried to put her finger on what was wrong with him. And out of the corner of her eye keeping in range the outline of Seamus Laffey by the door. Talking with some of the lads and pretending he was ignoring her, just as she was letting on she didn't see him. She liked Seamus. A lot. Though not passionately. At least not in the way she understood great passion from her literary readings. But she definitely liked him a lot more than she liked Timmy Mulligan. The problem was, he was as poor as a church mouse. It was a real conundrum. She liked Seamus enough to marry him if he had a bit of money. But not with enough passion to say the hell with comfort. On the other hand, Timmy Mulligan could support her in great style.

"They say 'twill be a great year for the wool," Timmy was saying. "The Australians had a drought, and that's always good for us." All he could talk about was wool and eggs and money. Even with his father lying dead up there in the bed.

"You'll miss your daddy," she said. Then there was the question of the Mulligan money. Could you save your immortal soul if you took it? Her mother was adamant that you couldn't. "Lord save us, Eileen, it's bad money and nothing it would buy you is worth the loss of your salvation."

"He'd been telling me to get married for some time," Timmy said, changing the subject. "'I want to see my grandson,' he'd say. I would have, too, if a certain person had been willing." Looking slyly out of the corner of his eye at her.

"I'm sure there are lots of girls who would be happy to oblige," she said. And there were. Timmy Mulligan was considered a prize catch. And he knew it. He had courted girls from Castlebar to Galway and back. Always girls from big farms or good shops: Martin Mulligan, it was well known, wanted his sons to marry money. Several times it was said that Timmy was on the verge of getting engaged. But always he would keep coming to see her. He'd drive back the boreen of an evening in the father's big Ford V8 and sit by the fire and talk with her mother. Sometimes you'd think it was Mammy he was courting instead of her. But he wasn't fooling Mammy. She'd always be polite to him, make the tea, and get down the currant cake. But after he'd leave she'd say, "I'd never have it on my conscience to take Mulligan money."

Eileen even raised the question with Father Coyne. Into the sacristy with her one Sunday after last mass and said she wanted a word with him in the house when he was ready. So he sat her down in his parlor and took off his biretta. "Well, what is it, my girl?"

"A question of conscience," she said.

"You've come to the right place, then." The parish priest settled back in an armchair. He loved nothing better than a good, juicy discussion.

"If someone came by money dishonestly and his son inherited it and the son was to marry someone, would it be wrong for that person to have the money and to spend it?" She was out of breath by the time she got that mouthful out.

"Stolen goods are stolen goods," Father Coyne intoned. "And the passing of time doesn't make honest what was gotten dishonestly." He put his hand in the pocket of his soutane and pulled out a penny. "If I steal money from a man's pocket and give it to you, do you have a right to spend it because *you* didn't steal it?" He put the penny on the table and his biretta back on his head as if to say the case was closed.

"When you put it as simple as that, Father, the answer is clear. But things are usually more complicated in real life." She had learned a bit of casuistry from the nuns, so he wasn't going to bamboozle her with a glib answer like that. "What if, for example, it's impossible to tell who the money was stolen from, or how much? And there's no way to return it without getting the person who took it into serious trouble. He might lose his business, and his family would starve. Now, what does he do?"

"He must find a way to make restitution." Father Coyne was unyielding as a stone wall. "There are ways, even in the sort of case you mention. You cannot retain ill-gotten goods and expect God's forgiveness."

"Suppose he gave some of the money he stole to the church to put up a statue or something? Would that be all right?" Which was what a lot of people had asked when Martin Mulligan donated the money for the lovely Calvary in front of Creevagh church.

The parish priest didn't bat an eyelid. "The church cannot accept ill-gotten gains any more than an individual person can." He took off the biretta again. "There must be moral certainty that any such money was not ill gotten. And that would be the case if the party in question had already made restitution for what was dishonestly come by."

More he wouldn't say, and Eileen didn't pursue the matter further. Though she still had her doubts that Martin Mulligan ever made restitution. And even greater concerns about Timmy Mulligan's qualifications as a husband. Not that he was too likely to ask her anyway, she thought at the time. His father would not approve.

Paddy Gannon wasn't the only one with an eye on Eileen Maille talking to Timmy Mulligan. Peter Solon, who killed the sheep for the mutton Martin Mulligan sold in his shop and packed the wool Martin Mulligan sold by the lorryload in Galway, was watching them too. More precisely, Peter was watching Timmy. With unfriendly bloodshot eyes. Peter Solon did not like Timmy Mulligan.

"I'm thinking I'll be off as soon as the funeral is over," Mark Gillespie was saying to Peter. A small, neat man Mark, who, unlike his big, awkward fellow worker, looked comfortable in a Sunday suit. It was Mark who handled the accounts for Martin Mulligan and tested the eggs that Timmy bought from the farmer's wives and packed those eggs into crates for shipment to Galway. "I'd dig ditches before I'd work for that fooking bastard."

"'Tis beyond my understanding," Peter said at the end of a long pull on his pint, "the way some people are born with money in their hands and the rest of us cannot come by it no matter how hard we work. I'm thinking sometimes that the Man Upstairs has His favorites too."

"Faith, He has strange taste if that fellow over there is one of them."

"I'd like to put my boot up his arse." Peter Solon tried to wiggle his toes, uncomfortable in Sunday shoes.

"I waited too long," said Mark. "In America I should have been years ago. I'd have money now. But himself had a way of getting you to stay. 'Mark,' he would say, 'sure, the whole bloody business would collapse if you walked out of here today.'"

"And you believed him," Peter Solon said, imbibing sympathetic porter.

"'I need more money,' I says to him. 'My mother is up there in Sligo living all by herself with only the old-age pension to keep her out of the poorhouse.' And Martin says, 'It isn't a lot more money you'd have in your pocket in England either after you paid for your digs and your passage back and forth to see your mother a couple of times a year.' 'I'd have more,' I says. 'You wouldn't, on me oath,' he says. 'Faith, I would,' I says. And we end up shouting at each other in the shop until herself comes in and wants to know what the row is all about. 'I'm going to England in the morning,' I says and walks out."

"But you didn't." Peter was understanding. "Me too. I was—"

"I hate England and all she stands for." There was always ferocity near the surface in Mark Gillespie. "The Tans shot my grandfather a month before I was born.

The only time I'll go to John Bull will be with a gun or a stick of dynamite. I'm going to America."

"The mother died last year, I remember." Peter Solon bowed his head. "The Lord have mercy on her."

"Himself was good to her." A suspicion of tears behind Mark Gillespie's thick-rimmed glasses. "After me telling him about her. A week later he comes when I'm packing eggs. 'Go visit your mother Sunday,' he says. 'Take the car.' During the war, mind you, when no one this side of Castlebar has petrol but himself. 'And bring a few things for her,' he says. He puts a sack of flour in the car. And sugar and tea and treacle and all kinds of things. I'm thinking he's gone soft in the head. And every couple of months the same thing. Right up to the day she died. How could you walk out on a man like that?"

"A hard man to figure out, that's for sure. He'd give you the shirt off his back if you needed it. But then he'd fight you for the penny if you didn't. I remember—"

"He says to me," the porter beginning to take effect on Mark, "'Gillespie, you're one hell of a brave man.' 'Why is that?' says I. 'Because,' he says, 'you have the courage of your convictions.' 'How so?' says I. 'Well,' he says, 'you're the only man in the entire parish of Creevagh who never goes to mass. Even the Yank Walsh, who told me himself on his solemn oath that he's an atheist, is on his knees inside the church door at Christmas and Easter.' 'There's no point in going,' I says to him, 'if you don't believe in it.' He just laughs at that. 'Faith, there's plenty of fellows in this parish who don't believe in it either, but they still walk up to the altar every month for the men's sodality. I'm one of them myself,' he says."

"Cripes!" Peter Solon slugged his porter for comfort.

"Do you think he meant it? He was a great man for pulling your leg."

"He said to me another time, 'Mark,' he says, 'I sometimes don't know why in God's name I get up in the morning.' He liked to watch me testing the eggs. 'And why is that?' I says. 'Because,' he says, 'the first thing I think of every morning is that this might be my last day on God's earth. And you know, some day it will be,' he says. 'And that's the God's truth, isn't it. So what's the point of doing anything?' he says."

"Well, wasn't he a terrible man," said Peter Solon.

"'But they'll remember Martin Mulligan,' he says. 'By God, they'll remember Martin Mulligan. I started without a penny in my pocket and now I'm the richest man in County Mayo, bar none. But you know something,' he says, 'I'm afraid of hell.'"

"Well, isn't that the divil and all," said Peter Solon.

"'Are you afraid of hell, Mark?' he says. And I says, 'Hell is an invention of those devils in black clothes to keep fellows like you and me from kicking over the traces.'"

"Speaking of the devil," said Peter Solon, nodding toward Father Coyne, who had just walked in through the kitchen and into the bedroom.

The parish priest knelt by the corpse for a long time. The conversation died down in the bedroom, as if talking might dilute the power of his prayer. When he got to his feet and blessed himself, he said loudly, as if addressing his congregation from the pulpit, "He was a fine man, the Lord have mercy on him." And straight over he went to Martin's wife, Clare, and shook her hand. A few people said Amen.

"It's a sad day for us all," said the priest to the widow.

"It is," she said, and dried a tear with a tiny lace handkerchief. "He was everyone's friend."

"He was. He was indeed." Father Coyne rubbed his hands. "Even his enemies liked him."

"Did Daddy have a lot of enemies?" Mona Mulligan asked, hanging on to her mother's arm. A tall, shy girl, youngest of the Mulligans, home from University College, Galway for the funeral.

"Sure, the man who wouldn't have a few enemies is not worth his salt," the parish priest said. "And your father was a great man, the Lord have mercy on him."

"He was a *good* man." Clare Mulligan could only whisper, overcome. "I don't know what I'll do without him."

"It's a cross," Father Coyne said comfortably. "A great cross to shoulder. But when God sends a cross he sends, too, the strength to carry it." And you could almost feel the courage in his words. Father Coyne was a great support to those in need.

"I suppose Paddy Gannon is one of those enemies," Mona said, her big eyes wide and she looking at the parish priest.

"Timmy and the boys know the business well," Father Coyne continued. "You won't have to worry about that part."

"Is he, Mammy?" Mona persisted. A terribly stubborn girl, the same Mona. Mr. Addis Emmet, the schoolmaster, said one time in exasperation to her father when she was only in fifth class, "She's as thin as a thrawneen, Martin, but when she makes up her mind to something she's as hard to move as an oak tree." That was the year before Addis Emmet and Martin Mulligan had the falling out after which they never spoke to each other again.

"Your father and Paddy Gannon had their disagreements." Clare Mulligan ran her hand lightly over her daughter's hair. "But I'd hardly say they were enemies."

"Why did they disagree?" Mona persisted. "Was it because Daddy cheated? That's what everyone says."

"Sure, 'tis water under the bridge now," said Father Coyne.

"I miss my daddy," the girl screamed suddenly and began to cry out loud. She rushed over to the bed and threw herself on it. "Daddy! Daddy! Why did you die? Come back! Do you hear me! Come back! I don't want you dead!" And then she blubbered. And then she screamed some more, disrupting the entire wake till all conversation stopped, even out in the parlor and the kitchen and the bar, everyone straining their necks to look in at the corpse and Mona Mulligan lying on top of it. "You had no right to die," she wailed. "You had no right to die."

And she screamed again, a piercing pitch that hurt Johnny Lydon's ears out in the bar on the far side of the kitchen. Very sensitive hearing Johnny had, ever since he was a child.

"When your time comes you go," Johnny said forcefully now to Thomas Ryan and Jack Higgins. "There's no call for this kind of carry-on."

"She'll miss him, the creature," Jack said. "They say she was his favorite."

"Faith, there's some of us won't miss him too much." Johnny Lydon looked at his empty tankard. "Maybe I'll have another one in his honor." Making his way half steadily over to the barrel on the counter.

"Bloody old hypocrite," Thomas Ryan remarked to his back. "Getting drunk at the expense of a man he never had the time of day for."

"It was he knew how to charge when he had the upper hand on you, by God. I remember," said Johnny, back with a fill of black porter, "I was looking for a bit of corrugated iron roof when Martin took down an old shed behind in the field. So I says to him, 'If you have no further use for that roof, I'll take it off your hands.' It was lying on the ground, so it was. Stopping the grass from growing. 'Faith, if you do,' he says, 'you'll pay me for it. That's a valuable roof.' 'It's rusted,' I says. 'I'm doing you a favor by taking it away.' But he wouldn't budge an inch. Two pounds he wanted. And I had to give it to him. Anyway, it was cheaper than buying a new one."

"It makes you think," Thomas Ryan, who was sipping Jameson, said to Jack Higgins, who wasn't drinking at all. "Martin Mulligan was ten years younger than me, and his time has already come."

"It's in the blood," Jack pronounced. "All the Mulligans died young. Yourself has good blood."

"I do, faith," Thomas agreed.

"But no one to pass it on to now," Johnny remarked as if speaking to an unseen person on his right.

Thomas Ryan sipped some more Jameson. Jack Higgins looked down at the floor. Everyone knew about Thomas's young wife, Catherine, who in more than five years of marriage hadn't given him a single child. And to crown it all, didn't she just recently leave him and run off to England. A terrible thing entirely, everyone said.

Though there were those miserable people who added, Why did he marry her in the first place, and he forty years older than her?

"'Tis hard to keep the women at home these days." Johnny seemed to be talking to himself.

"They say you're going for the Dail at the next election," Thomas Ryan said loudly to Jack Higgins. "You'll make a fine T.D., I'm thinking. We need a man like yourself up there. The country is going to the dogs these days."

"What is it coming to at all," Johnny Lydon said, "when a man can't drink a pint anymore with all the tax the government is putting on it? You'll take care of that, now, when you get up there, Jack?" He winked slyly at Thomas Ryan.

"I have to get there first." Jack turning suddenly solemn and humble. "'Tis no easy thing to do when you're a small farmer like myself."

"What small farmer?" said Johnny, looking shocked. "Sure, you'd buy and sell the lot of us and not miss it. And you're a county councilor as well!"

"I was counting on himself a great deal," Jack said confidentially, nodding in the general direction of the corpse. "He knew everyone. And what's more, everyone owed him something. That always helps when you want to get the vote. But it's all gone now." He dug his hands deeper into his trousers pockets and resumed his contemplation of the floor.

"You'll do well with the farmers," Thomas said. "The farmers are the backbone of this county, and they're tired of having fellows up there in Dublin talking for them that wouldn't know one end of a cow from the other. You stand up on your soapbox outside the churches on Sunday mornings and tell them you're a small farmer like themselves and you understand their problems, and they'll vote for you to a man. And it won't matter whether they're Fianna Fail or Fine Gael or Clann na Talmhan. 'Tis the farmer in you they'll be voting for."

"Begob," Johnny said, the porter coursing comfortably through his veins, "you'd make a bloody fine Teachta Dala yourself, Thomas. Wouldn't he now, Jack?"

"Martin Mulligan once told me," Jack Higgins said, "that if you promised the farmers two pounds more for every wether they sold and five pounds more for every bullock, they'd give you every vote they had."

"Faith, I'd vote for a man who could do that for me," Johnny Lydon put in in a hurry.

"You could promise them that," Thomas Ryan agreed. "You could promise them ten pounds, for that matter. But could you deliver on your promise?"

"He didn't say you had to deliver," Jack Higgins noted. "He only said you could promise it. 'It's a fair bet,' he used to say. What he meant was that in the normal course of events nowadays you can expect prices to go up that much between elections regardless of who wins. So you might as well take the credit for it. If *you* don't, the other fellow will."

Mona Mulligan shrieked again. Johnny Lydon winced and pulled hard on his pint. "Women are damnable creatures," he said.

"They are," Jack Higgins unexpectedly agreed. There seemed to be a bit of fervor in his assent.

"Your wife will be a great asset to you as a T.D., I'm thinking," said Thomas. "She has a power of a tongue in her head, and she knows how to use it." But there was a bleakness in his tone that belied any notion of compliment. Thomas Ryan had his own suspicions that the tongue of Maura Higgins was no small factor in the disappearance of his own Catherine a few months back.

Those suspicions might have been strengthened if he could have overheard the conversation going on that very minute in the next room between the same Maura Higgins and Eileen Maille. Maura had stepped in between Eileen and Timmy Mulligan without so much as a by your leave, and Timmy left in a hurry. He couldn't stand the living sight of Maura Higgins.

"Is Daddy's little boy still pestering you?" Maura asked.

"He's not Daddy's little boy anymore," said Eileen. "He owns the place now."

"What's that supposed to mean?" Maura cocked a quizzical, tell-me-everything eyebrow. She and Eileen were thick as thieves.

"Now that Daddy is dead, he came right out and asked me."

"To marry him?"

"No less. Would you believe it?"

"You can't be serious? You mean right here, just now?"

"In this very spot." Eileen seemed to be blushing.

"With the old man hardly cold up in the bed!"

"Sensitivity was never one of Timmy's strong points."

"I wish I could have heard him propose. Dear God! It must have been wicked. Did he do it like Clark Gable?

Go down on one knee? 'My darling!' Maura tried to look solemn but let a guffaw escape before she could suppress it. This was not the place for laughing. "Excuse me," she said. "It's just . . ."

"I'm giving it some serious thought," Eileen said seriously.

Maura Higgins instantly acquired the confused look of a woman unexpectedly kicked by a horse. Her facial muscles received so many simultaneous contradictory commands that they twitched and wiggled as if dancing a jig. Several times in seconds her mouth opened to speak but closed in silence. Finally she managed, "You mean you're thinking of marrying him?"

"Well, he's not half bad-looking at all," Eileen said defiantly.

"He's not," Maura agreed quickly, too quickly. "He's the best-looking eejit this side of Castlebar if money and a long nose are what you're looking for. He . . . Stop! Stop, Maura Higgins! Shut your mouth, girl, and say no more," Maura Higgins said and shut her mouth.

There was silence between them. Maura with her eyes on the wall and Eileen looking towards the door where Seamus Laffey had been but was no longer. In the end Eileen said, "Talk to me, Maura. I'm all mixed up. I don't know what I'm doing."

Maura said, "Do you want me to tell you to go ahead and marry him? Or do you want me to tell you what I think?"

Eileen looked like she was about to cry. "I don't know. Tell me what you think. You think I'm daft, I know. But I'm tired of living hand to mouth. Do you have any idea how little bank clerks get paid? I'd like to drive around in a V8 car and wear a fur coat in the winter. Do you know what I mean?"

"Catherine Ryan found out that money wasn't everything."

"That was different. Thomas Ryan is as old as Methuselah. Timmy is my own age."

"Okay! So you're Mrs. Timothy Mulligan. And it's twelve o'clock at night. And you step out of your V8 motorcar. And you take off your fur coat. And you get into bed beside your husband. Timothy Patrick Mulligan. The richest man in Creevagh. And his hands are roaming all over you, in places mentionable and unmentionable. How are you feeling?"

"Maura! I'm almost a virgin yet."

"You take a couple of spins in the V8 with Timmy, girl, and you won't be one for long. It isn't known how many girls have been introduced to that fellow's appendage in the back seat of his car."

"You're awful, Maura Higgins."

"There have been consequences more than once, too, let me tell you. Martin Mulligan has paid good money to keep things quiet."

"I think I'm going to cry," Eileen Maille said, and she did.

"It's all right." Maura Higgins took a tiny handkerchief out of her purse and gave it to her friend. "They'll think you're crying for Martin."

That made both of them giggle and put an end to Eileen's tears.

"What am I going to do?" Eileen wiping her eyes with Maura's handkerchief.

"If you want my advice, you won't get married at all.

Not to mind to Timmy Mulligan. You're looking at someone who's been married for ten years. And to a man that everyone said was a great catch at that. Well, let me tell you. The whole institution is a great big bollix. Pace Father Coyne and his sermons on the sacrament and the need for young men to get married. It's the men he's talking to. Maybe he knows something about their needs. But he knows nothing at all about women, I can tell you that."

Maura took a sip of her Scotch and made a face. "It's terrible stuff, but if they can drink it, so can I. Anyway, you cease to exist as a person in your own right from the moment you put on that ring. He owns you lock, stock, and barrel as soon as he takes you home. You're like a prize cow. Something to be shown off and admired. To make other men envious. To be used like a prize cow too. A baby every year and soon you begin to look and act and feel like a cow. Except a cow can wean her calves after a few months: you're stuck with yours for life. Once a mother, forever a mother: you have no other life till the day you die."

"How did you manage . . . I mean . . . to avoid . . ." Eileen Maille blushed with embarrassment.

"Nature," said Maura Higgins obligingly. "His or mine. Who knows? Of course everyone assumes it's mine. But I've done a bit of reading on the matter. He wanted me to have tests done, you see. I said, 'I will if you do too.' Well! My dear! You never heard such carry-on. Is it him subject his you-know-what to tests? Not on your life. But it's perfectly all right for them—men, male doctors—to prod and poke and inspect my most private innards as if I was the aforesaid cow. I said to him, 'How would you like your prize possessions to be the subject of personal scrutiny by a couple of female doctors? Who just might end up by telling you that you don't have what it takes.' He didn't like that at all, I can tell you. But he never suggested I go for tests again."

"You're a riot, Maura Higgins," Eileen Maille said. "I wish I was like you."

"You don't want to be like me. I think too much. I know too much. It doesn't make for a peaceful existence. Maybe the women who have babies every year are better off. They don't seem to be too unhappy, hunched over their washboards half the time and feeding children and pigs and chickens the other half."

"With Timmy . . ."

"I know. I know. You'd have a maid to do the drudge. And that helps. But you're not your own person anymore. You're Mrs. Timothy Mulligan—call me Timmy. I'm Mrs. Jack Higgins." Maura suddenly leaned over and whispered, "This is for you only. For God's sake, don't tell anyone. I'm seriously thinking of leaving Jack."

"Jesus, Mary, and Joseph, you can't mean it?" Eileen's eyes wide with the shock.

"Mind you, Jack is not a bad man. In many ways I like him. It's the politics I can't stand. The posturing and the dishonesty and the jockeying for power. Ever since he became a county councilor. He was a lovely man before he got himself into it. Now . . . And your man up in the bed it was started it all."

"I thought it was Jack's idea. To be the great Mayo politician or whatever."

"He came home one night and said Mulligan wanted him to run for the county council. That's how it all got started. Martin didn't want to run himself because it might hurt the business on him. But you know who pulls the strings. Or did, anyway, until yesterday morning. God forgive me, I find it hard to even say a prayer for his soul."

"Well," said Eileen the consoler, "maybe things will be different now."

"No. It's on to the Dail now. Martin Mulligan's legacy to his protégé, Jack Higgins. And the last straw for me. If he runs I'm out."

"But you'd be a T.D.'s wife, Maura! Having a great time up in Dublin meeting all the important people and going to parties and all kinds of things."

"I never thought I'd see the day," Maura Higgins breathed rather than said. Staring left of the pearl on Eileen Maille's right ear. "Addis bloody Emmet and the missus! Did you ever?"

Addis Emmet did not come lightly to Martin Mulligan's wake. He had spent the day in a state of distracted indecision. A blessing for those of his scholars who had neglected to memorize their allotted lines of poetry. The young wastrels had warmed their palms in advance by sitting on them. And duly stumbled and stalled when asked to recite. But the schoolmaster's eyes were glazed and his reflexes failed and he never once reached into his drawer for the leather strap. Addis Emmet hated Martin Mulligan. A deep, fierce detestation of the blackguard simmered without cease on the hearth of his mind. Whenever the man's name was so much as mentioned in his presence, the simmering bubbled to a boil. There would be no forgiveness for what Mulligan had said and done as long as he, Addis Emmet, was alive. And if he had to go to hell for his hate, he once said to himself in a moment of extraordinary virulence, so be it. So when he heard of the ruffian's demise on his way out of mass Sunday morning, he said immediately to Mrs. Emmet, "Good riddance of a bad lot." And he didn't care who heard him.

"Addis!" She was shocked. The kindest woman in the parish, Mrs. Emmet. "May the Lord have mercy on his soul," she said with fervor.

"May the devil take him," retorted Addis. "I intend," he added, "to pass the rest of my days on my bended knees so I won't spend eternity in the same place as that bloody scoundrel."

So why he came to the wake was a mystery even to himself. "We'll go, then," he said out of the blue to Mrs. Emmet after she put away the dinner things.

"Go where?" She took *Pride and Prejudice* from the dresser and her reading glasses from the pocket of her apron and sat wearily in her chair by the fire.

"To that blackguard's wake."

"Martin Mulligan, is it? The Lord have mercy on him." She removed her glasses to see what was wrong with her spouse. "What's got into you at all?"

"We'll go now," he said, getting up abruptly out of his chair.

"You said you wouldn't be found dead inside his house." But she got up anyway. You didn't argue with Addis when he was in that kind of mood.

"He's the one that's dead inside his house," he said, and she thought the look on his face almost orgasmic.

Addis and Mrs. knelt by the side of Martin Mulligan's deathbed. Both praying in their own ways for his departed soul. Mrs. said, "O merciful God, have pity on your servant Martin Mulligan. They say he did bad things, but who are we to judge? And what does it matter now? Punishing people doesn't serve any purpose, does it, Lord? So forgive him his sins and bring him into everlasting life. And grant my husband the grace to forgive him too." She would have blessed herself and risen then but Addis was still on his knees with his eyes closed.

Addis prayed, "O God, don't ever let this wretched sinner stand before your throne of grace. His like has not been seen in Ireland since Oliver Cromwell crossed the land. Send him to join cursed Oliver in the deep, dark dungeons of hell. He had no right, O Lord! He had no right. A lifetime, I spent, Sweet Jesus, in building my name. Till I was the most respected man, not only in the parish of Creevagh, but in half the county. And he destroyed it. What is a man without his honor and his good name? If you take them away, you have taken his life. Martin Mulligan, cursed be he forever, took away my life. It is not so, Lord. Say it is not so. My sainted mother could not have conceived me except in Thy grace. In Thy grace I was born and have always lived. And in Thy grace I will die."

It was at this point that Mrs. Addis, glancing sideways, wondering at the length of her husband's prayer, saw his eyes squeeze shut and his jaw close tight like a child who had just swallowed cod liver oil. She wanted to nudge him but you didn't nudge Addis Emmet in public, not even if you were his wife of twenty years. So she stayed on her knees, and Addis stayed at his prayers. "Sweet Jesus, I will not forgive him. Don't ask me, please. I will go to Lough Derg and do the stations ten times on my bended knees. I will climb Croagh Patrick in the blinding rain. But Martin Mulligan I will not forgive. He said it in front of everyone. And you can never take back what is said, no matter how false it is. And so you can never forgive what is unforgivably said, no matter how long after, not even when the liar is dead. It wasn't as if I had insulted him. All I did was remark that some people seemed to profit from the misery of others. Him and his black market tea in the middle of a war, and people going hungry. So what call did he have to say what he did? And three people in the shop at the time. All with cocked ears for what schoolmaster and shopkeeper would say so they could carry it home and repeat it and repeat it till the slightest remark was a statement of import and the snidest innuendo was gospel forever. 'None of us is perfect,' he remarks. A truth we all know and that didn't need preaching. 'Especially those who are born too soon,' he says. And the wink in his piggy little eyes. And the smirk across his ugly puss. Oh, they all knew what he meant, though no one said anything. Pretending not to be listening. But you can be sure they heard it and understood it and went home to tell it to everyone they met. And they're laughing to this day at Mr. Addis Emmet, the bastard schoolmaster. I see it in their eyes. I hear it in their tones. I am no longer their rock of honor and truth and respectability."

"Are you done?" Mrs. whispered out of the corner of her mouth. A behavior she never tolerated in her pupils. But she could bear the prayer of her husband no longer. People were beginning to look, she thought. And the volume of conversation was diminishing, it seemed. But Addis did not acknowledge her question. His scrunched-up face and supplicating posture were as rigid as the corpse in the bed. Were it not for Mona Mulligan letting loose another piteous shriek of despair and hurling herself anew on her father's corpse, the schoolmaster might have spent the night there on his knees hurling fierce and silent imprecations against his departed detractor. As it was, he took advantage of the disturbance to slip out as quietly as he had come in, with only a nod in the direction of Father Coyne, still engaged in consoling the widow.

"'Tis a mystery to me," Father Coyne said, "why two such fine men as your husband and Addis Emmet haven't spoken to each other for years."

"It is," Clare Mulligan, said, trying to ignore the commotion her daughter was causing. "I asked Martin about it once, and he said he didn't know. 'One day he was talking to me,' he said, 'and the next day he wasn't.' He doesn't speak to me either, and I never did anything to him. Mrs. always says hello, mind you, and stops for a few words now and again, but you get the feeling she's looking over her shoulder all the while."

"You never know what's going on inside Addis's head," the priest said. It was not the kind of remark he would normally make: Father Coyne was very careful about commenting on any of his parishioners, because of the seal and the danger of giving scandal, you see. But he and Clare were good friends for a long time. There were even a few gossipmongers who said they were maybe a little too great with each other, but there was no call at all for slander of that sort. They were just on the kind of terms that allowed them to call a spade a spade. Even a parish priest needed a friend like that. And God knows the like were hard to find in the parish of Creevagh.

"Martin, God rest him, didn't let on too much either. And sometimes, to tell you the truth, I wouldn't want to know what he was up to. Was that wrong of me, Father?"

"Arrah, why would it be wrong! You always did your duty, and you followed your conscience. What more could be expected of you? We cannot be held accountable for what other people do. Even if it's our own flesh and blood."

And 'twas as well she didn't know, was what Father Coyne was thinking. He did indeed have a soft spot for Clare Mulligan. The finest woman he knew. But married to a prime blackguard. The dimensions of which he himself could hardly have guessed until Mulligan's last confession on Friday night. Of course he had known something about the black market. Everyone did. Especially those who had paid Martin Mulligan thirty shillings a pound for tea during the war. Mulligan had even confessed it several years ago when he decided, as he said, to turn over a new leaf and take care of his immortal soul. And he made restitution, he said, to those he cheated by putting extra weight in everybody's pound of tea for a whole year. The hypocrite! And he, Father Tom Coyne, guardian of morals for the parish of Creevagh and Kilsaggart, had taken him at his word. And taken, too, the money that Mulligan said was honestly made. And used it to build that beautiful Calvary for the edification of the people of Creevagh. And thought no more about it. Until last Friday night.

"I'm dying, Father," Mulligan rasped the moment the priest walked into the room. Querulously, as if he were complaining that the price of eggs had dropped.

"Indeed he's not," Clare said, in a chair by the bed knitting. "He's got this notion, Father. Tell him he's going to be all right."

"And why did you send for himself, then?" Mulligan's cough was like stones tumbling off a wall. Clare dropped a hand from the knitting to put a handkerchief on his mouth so he could spit into it. "When the priest comes to anoint you, it's all over bar the shouting. Amn't I right, Father?"

"Well, now, Martin, this is just a precaution. Extreme Unction is the anointing of the sick, you see. And one of its properties is to heal the body as well as the soul."

"Well, isn't the church a wonderful institution, Father," Mulligan said. "It has something for every occasion."

"I'll leave you now, Father, to hear his confession." Clare rolled up her thread and headed for the door.

"Divil a much I have to confess," the sick man said loudly. "Amn't I at confession and communion every week!" But Clare closed the door behind her, and Father Coyne sat in her chair.

"Am I dying, Father? Tell me the God's honest truth, now. Women, you know, will never tell you. But I'd trust you, Father." He ran thin fingers lightly across his eyes. There was no doubt he had failed an awful lot in the past month since he got sick. "No one ever wants to tell a man that he's dying. Isn't that strange, Father? But I want to know. A man should know. The biggest day in your life, and no one wants to let on. So tell me now."

"The doctor says you mightn't have too long. But then doctors have been known to be wrong."

"I knew it, damn them! Excuse the French, Father. I

knew it! You can't fool Martin Mulligan. Even when he's on his last legs. They wouldn't say it to my face, blast them. But I knew it." His pupils rolled away under the eyelids as if he were communicating with some unseen being. "You can't pull the wool over Martin Mulligan's eyes."

"If there's anything bothering you now, Martin, just tell it. Himself is merciful." It was Father Coyne's favorite comforting pronouncement before a last confession. He took the purple stole from his pocket and put it around his neck. "So go ahead with you, now."

"Ah, sure, the divil a much I have to tell you, Father. Bless me, Father, for I have sinned. I confess . . ." But then the stones began tumbling again, and he heaved and shuddered with the struggle to get some air into his lungs. He started again: "I confess to . . ."

"Don't mind the Confiteor now," the priest said. "Just the essentials."

"There isn't much of that either, Father. You don't have time for sin when you're on the broad of your back getting ready to face your Maker. I shouted at the missus a couple of times maybe. I'm a terrible man for the shouting, Father. Sure, you know that. And 'tis hard to break the habit of a lifetime."

"Very good. Very good. Anything else?"

"Ah, sure, why would there, Father? The man under the covers down here doesn't give you much trouble when you're trying hard just to breathe."

"And there's nothing at all from your past life?" Perfunctory question. Asked out of habit.

"The past is all behind me, Father. I'm ready to meet Himself."

"I'll give you absolution, then. Make a good act of contrition."

"There's maybe just one small thing, Father. Sure, I have a terrible memory altogether. I had them all searching the house for my cap the other day, and wasn't it on my head all the time."

"I see. Well, I'm sure the Good Lord will overlook that. A good act of contrition now."

"I might have forgot to tell you everything about the black market."

"You told me it all before, Martin. And you made restitution as well. It's all forgiven. Say the—"

"'Tis likely I didn't tell you it all, Father."

The dying, with their scruples and their fears, as they get closer to their Maker. "I'm sure you did your best now. And that's all God expects from us."

"Will you stop and listen to me, Father?" With a great effort Martin Mulligan sat up in the bed. "It wasn't just what I sold in the shop and that I told you about. I made thousands of pounds carrying all sorts of black market merchandise down from Dublin and selling it to half the shopkeepers of Mayo at a roaring profit. A power of money entirely. What do you think paid for your Calvary?"

"Mother of God! And you didn't confess this before or make restitution?"

"Why would I be telling you now if I did? It's only just the other day I thought of it as a sin. Isn't it strange, Father, a lot of the things in life that you look on as bad later on didn't seem wrong at all when you were doing them. Isn't that funny, now?"

They said it was the most beautiful Calvary in the

West of Ireland, was all the priest could think of at that
minute.

"And that's why I didn't tell you before, Father."

"I see," Father Coyne said.

The dying man grabbed the priest's arm. "You won't
have Timmy make restitution now, Father, so you won't?
He doesn't know a thing about it. And that's the God's
honest truth. Why would he? He was only a nipper at the
time."

"Does the missus know?" The question, the priest
faintly perceived, was more personal than pastoral.

"Arrah, why would she?" Mulligan slumped back on
the pillow. "Clare asks no questions, Father, and I tell her
no lies. Sure, you know her yourself as well as I do."

"You'll have to promise now that when you get better
you'll go about making restitution in this matter."

"Oh I will, Father. I certainly will. You can set your
mind easy on that."

The priest bowed his head. "Is there anything else?"

"But I'm forgiven now, Father? Amn't I?"

"Providing you're sincerely sorry, yes. Make a good
act of contrition now."

"And if I die before I can make restitution, Timmy is
free and clear, isn't he, Father?"

"Well, now, if he becomes aware of it he will have an
obligation. You can't . . ."

"Ah, but who's to tell him, Father? Only you and I
know. And the seal of confession can't be broken. Isn't
that right, Father?"

"He provided well for us," Clare Mulligan was saying.

"He did indeed." But a sort of spiritual nausea came
over Father Coyne. As if he had eaten something unsa-

vory. The image of Martin Mulligan's face when he gave him absolution. And the Calvary he was so proud of. He'd like to take a hammer to it this minute. "I'll go home now and finish my breviary."

It was raining again. He was turning up the collar of his coat outside the door when Paddy Gannon said from behind, "Could I have a word with you, Father? I'll walk up to the house with you."

"To be sure, Paddy." Though the last thing he wanted was to talk to anyone at that moment. "I've been meaning to have a chat with you one of these days."

"I haven't been to confession for fifteen years," the publican said humbly, and they walking up the road.

"Is that so, now?" But well he knew it. In his curate days of intemperate zeal, he'd have badgered the man into the box. But the years had made him wiser.

"It was hate, Father, that kept me away. I hated a man enough to go to hell for the pleasure of it. God won't forgive your sins, they say, while you hate someone. Isn't that true, Father?"

"That's true, for sure."

"Well, I hated Martin Mulligan, Father. God damn him to hell."

"We must forgive those who do us wrong, just as we hope to be forgiven."

"I never fornicated with *his* daughter, like he did with mine."

"Mother of God!" Father Coyne couldn't help it. "Your daughter is in America, isn't she?"

"That's what everyone thinks. But she's up in Dublin rearing his bastard, that's where she is."

"Indeed! Is that so?"

"The lad is fifteen, Father. Martin was paying for his keep. And I want that to go on. And more. He's Martin Mulligan's son, the same as Timmy and the rest of them and he has a right to his share of the Mulligan money."

It's tainted money, was what Father Coyne, if it weren't for the seal of confession, would have told Paddy Gannon at that minute.

"You'll help me get it for him, Father?"

Now what would the theologians have to say about that? was what flashed through the priest's mind. "Well, I don't know if it's my place to interfere, now, Paddy. I'm on your side, mind you, but I don't think it would be appropriate, as it were, for me to say anything. Maybe it were best if you hired a solicitor."

"I could do that, Father. And maybe I will yet." Paddy Gannon stopped several paces from the door of the priest's house. "You're good friends with Mrs. Mulligan, Father. Maybe you'd put in a word with her. If I go to a solicitor the whole county will know. But sure, nobody wants that to happen, now do they, Father?"

In the dark Paddy Gannon couldn't see the ever so fleeting trace of a smile that crossed the parish priest's face. "No, Paddy, nobody would want that to happen." Then Father Coyne's tone became that of stern confessor. "Restitution must be made, and it will be made. You just leave it to me. I'll discuss the matter with Timmy as soon as the funeral is over. Your grandson will get his fair share of the Mulligan wealth. But not a word to Clare, mind you. We wouldn't want to cause more pain to the poor woman."

"I'll be at confession for the men's sodality," Paddy Gannon promised. "Good night to you now, Father."

The

Communist

Threat

I N THE summer of 1953 Communism was on everyone's mind. Communism with a capital C. The yellow peril rolling westward in countless numbers from faraway Korea and China, the hordes of Russians and their East European minions straining at the Iron Curtain, struck a remote fear even into the parish of Creevagh. The apocalyptic warnings of its threat to civilization, uttered by Senator Joseph McCarthy in the Congress of the United States of America, were reported not only in the *Irish Press* and the *Irish Independent* but through the voice of Radio Eireann reverberating around the kitchens of Creevagh parish. Not to mention Gannon's and Mulligan's public houses, where the ten o'clock news was listened to and freely discussed over the final Guinness before closing time.

Father Coyne's Sunday sermons brought home the immediacy of the global menace: "Let it not be thought," he thundered, "that this atheistic propaganda cannot penetrate the sacred portals of holy Ireland. It can, and it has. There are even those in our midst here in this very parish who are infected with the awful creed of anti-Christ. They propagate heretical doctrines, they refuse to listen to their priest and they even reject the authority of Holy Mother Church herself."

Those in the know knew that the "they" to whom he referred was singular: to wit, Maura Higgins, wife to county councilor Jack Higgins. The woman had become extremely outspoken over the past couple of years on social and political affairs. It was said that it was on account of her and her wagging tongue that Jack, as staunch a capitalist as you could find in all of County Mayo, had not been elected to Dail Eireann in the last general election. Wasn't she a big supporter of Dr. Noel Browne's mother and child scheme, a Communist plot that, if ever there was one? But a plot that failed because the people of holy Ireland, ably led by their cardinal, bishops, and priests, recognized it for what it was and brought down the government that supported it. That defeat had embittered Maura Higgins no end. "A crowd of antediluvian Neanderthals," was how she characterized both clergy and populace to Eileen Maille one morning after examining the latest headlines in the *Irish Times*. She was the only person in the parish who read that Protestant West Briton newspaper, according to

Timmy Mullligan, who should know since he was the only one who had it for sale. And everyone knew that the *Times* was partial to Communism.

Eileen wasn't quite sure what Maura's words meant, though she understood clearly that they were not complimentary. Anyway, she was getting married to Timmy in September and her mind was on other things.

"You're always into something, Maura Higgins," she said. "Maybe you should run for the Dail yourself next time." She was really wondering if there would be any problem about the Higginses coming to the wedding, given the bad blood between Maura and Father Coyne.

"I know one thing I'm not doing," Maura said. "I'm never going near that bloody place again." They were standing outside Mulligan's Bar, Victuals, and Grocery and she was pointing down the street at the parish church.

"You'll come to see me married, won't you?" Eileen was almost wailing. It was going to be the biggest splash Creevagh parish had ever seen, Timmy said, and it was important that the county councilor be there.

"I'll make an exception for you," Maura promised. "But that's it for the rest of my life."

Phelim O'Brien heard the latest about Maura Higgins from Seamus Laffey the day after he arrived home for the holidays. He was sitting on the wall in front of the house meditating on the Passion of Christ, a practice he had grown very fond of during the thirty-day Ignatian Exercises he had just completed, when he saw his friend slouching back the road towards him. There was an awfully sad look on Laffey's face. "What in the name of all that's holy is the matter with you?" Phelim asked.

Seamus Laffey right there and then put his hands up to his face and cried like a baby. Such blubbering you never saw: convulsing and bawling and sniveling and snot. Poor Phelim didn't know whether to get sick himself or go for Dr. Daly, so he just hopped down from the wall and waited for the exhibition to end, the way you wait for a wild horse to stop galloping around a field before going after him with a bridle. After a while Seamus calmed down and wiped his nose with his sleeve. "Sorry," he managed a couple of times before the second wave swept over him. This time he leaned his backside against the wall to ride it out.

Eventually he pulled himself together enough to anathematize Timmy Mulligan in no uncertain language. Eileen Maille—*his* Eileen—marrying that bloody bugger. The fecking hoor, the scamp, the blackguard: the entire litany of vilification, including everything foul that Mulligan had ever perpetrated from the day of his birth to the present moment. Somewhere near the end of the diatribe he mentioned Maura Higgins's row with Father Coyne, a tragedy he also attributed to Timothy's wickedness.

"What did Maura do this time?" Phelim asked, both in an attempt to deflect Seamus from further vituperation and because he well knew Mrs. Higgins's propensity for uncommon causes.

"She's a Communist! Father Coyne says she's a Communist. I think Mulligan is one too," he added, suddenly realizing that he had omitted this slur from his list.

"Is that a fact?" Phelim's ears went back with the tightening of his face. The word "Communist" always did that to him. He had very strong feelings about this twentieth-century plague on mankind. It was a subject on which he had meditated long and intensely and about which he had received a personal message from the Sacred Heart on the Feast of Corpus Christi last year to the effect that his great priestly mission in life would be to combat this modern manifestation of Satan incarnate.

"She won't listen to a word Father Coyne says," Laffey noted. "And she doesn't even go to mass anymore. Mulligan is always *late* for last mass," he added gratuitously.

"I see." Phelim stared west towards the blue Mweelrea Mountains, with the cone top of Croagh Patrick sticking up behind them. "It's best that I talk to her, then," he said sagely. But he said no more. The profound nature of his lecture to the parish Communist was not something that a simple layman like Seamus Laffey would be likely to understand. Maura, on the other hand, was known to be a fierce brain altogether, and although Phelim rarely exchanged more than the most perfunctory of greetings with her, he recognized immediately that the path to capturing her soul lay through her intellect. That would be where Father Coyne had failed. A good priest, mind you, but Phelim had detected in a conversation with him last year a great lack of interest in the intellectual underpinnings of the faith. Which was all very well when you were dealing with simple farmers, but smart people like Maura Higgins needed a bit of theology to shape their beliefs. And Phelim O'Brien was the man to provide that, if he might say so himself. After only one year of theological studies he was already, he could say in all modesty, beginning to be recognized as one of the best theological minds in Kimmage. This was particularly true in the areas of canon law and moral, where his keen brain could split in two even the finest of casuistic distinctions. There was indeed some talk that he might be sent to Rome after ordination to get a doctorate, though he himself took no part in such immodest speculation. Add to his theological knowledge his profound studies in dialectical materialism during his last year at the university, he reminded himself, and you had here a man well prepared to convince Maura Higgins of the errors of her ways.

He needed only the opportunity. After mass on Sunday would be the obvious time, but of course the woman was no longer going to mass. And he didn't really know her well enough to cycle back to her house without an excuse. As it happened, he found the excuse coming out of mass anyway. Walking out the church gate on Sunday morning he spotted a torn old election poster hanging from the wall right across the road. It had Jack Higgins's picture on it, and underneath in large letters it said:

VOTE FOR JACK HIGGINS
THE MAN WHO LISTENS TO YOU

On Monday evening Phelim leaned his bike against the wall of the Higgins's front garden on the Kilmolara road, opened the fancy wrought-iron gate, and walked firmly up the concrete path to the front door. He'd like to talk with Jack, he said.

"Unfortunately, Jack is not at home at the moment." Mrs. Higgins stood squarely in the doorway, not inviting him in, giving him about as much attention as a cattle jobber would devote to a scrawny bullock at the fair of Kilmolara.

"Maybe yourself can help me, then." The words came out of his mouth unbidden, entirely against the legacy of advice from all holy men of the past to all practicing celibates of the present about not spending time alone in the company of women. In his defense it can be said that at that precise moment he hardly noticed that this gorgeous woman's dress had no sleeves or that the front of it was open a third of the way down for want of buttoning or that it came only to her knees or that she was barefoot. His mind was entirely occupied with the opportunity God had just put in his way of turning this atheist back to the true faith. "In what way?" But she made no move to ask him in.

He was intending to write a paper on a social and moral question of great importance to the country, he explained, staring past her at the brass knocker that badly needed polishing, and he wanted to get the views of an intelligent politician like Jack Higgins on the subject. However, since he wasn't home, maybe herself might be interested in talking about it.

"I might." She stood looking at him for a long time without so much as a word out of her. He looked down at the steps, more, it must be admitted, out of embarrassment than from obedience to the holy rule that called for rigorous custody of the eyes when in the presence of the opposite sex. Finally she said, "Come in." It was a lovely house. Flowered wallpaper in the hallway. Shiny mahogany and brightly upholstered furniture in the parlor. A piano. A carpet on the floor. Paintings on the walls. Though, mind you, there was a lot of dust everywhere, a state of affairs that would never be tolerated in the scholasticate. "Make yourself at home." She pointed to an armchair. And she sat opposite him on a sofa and crossed her legs, raising the dress to facilitate the movement. God help him, he couldn't help but notice, and it was a terrible distraction that made him forget what he was about to say for the moment.

"I only met Jack once or twice," he babbled. "He's a nice man."

"He is." And she crossed her legs the other way, this time keeping an eye on him as if daring him to look.

"I'm writing a paper," he began, and then had to clear his throat. He was feeling very uncomfortable with the look she was giving him: it had none at all of that friendly deference he was accustomed to receiving from friends and neighbors ever since he had started coming home wearing a Roman collar. "I'm writing a paper about Communism and the welfare state, you see."

"Oh!" she said, and in that one word he knew he had her attention. "Is that a fact? Well, now, there's a subject that's dear to my own heart, I must say." And again she did her ceremonial raising of dress and crossing of bare white legs. This time his eyes would not stay away despite his best effort. He noticed there was a light brown fuzz of hair on her shins, and he felt himself blushing.

"They're both a serious threat to the spiritual well-being of this country," he pronounced, and to his credit he managed to say it with a certain touch of authority. The scholastic training showed.

"Arrah, they're no such thing." There was real annoyance in her instant retort. She leaned away back in the sofa and locked her fingers behind her head. The dress slid high over her knees. "That's a lot of nonsense!"

The way she fell for the bait so easily brought him

great satisfaction. "The papal encyclicals have all been very clear on the subject," he pointed out almost smugly. He was on home ground now.

"Feck the papal encyclicals." She leaned forward, elbows resting on bare knees and chin cupped in her hands. "How much money do *you* earn every week?"

He knew the top of the dress was gaping open, but to give him his due, he managed to refrain from looking in. "I'm a Scholastic." He was trying hard to remain calm in the face of such blasphemous irreverence. "I'm studying to be a priest. I don't earn money. As a matter of fact I have a vow of poverty," he added, cleverly anticipating where the question was leading.

"So who's feeding you, then? Who's putting that suit you're wearing on your back? Who's paying for your studies?" She leaned back again, crossing the legs and folding the arms. There was a cold, even antagonistic gleam in her eye.

"The people of Ireland!" He said it grandly and with pride. "Rich and poor alike. They value their priests, and they gladly pay for their training and upkeep. The Lord ordained that they who preach the gospel should live by the gospel. It was St. Paul himself who said that," he added portentously.

"Feck St. Paul." She said it calmly, without changing the expression on her face one iota. "The fact is you're being fed and dressed and housed and educated by a welfare state, the people of Ireland, and now you want to bite the hand that feeds you."

The argument was obviously spurious, although he had not come across it before. So it was his turn to say, "That's a lot of nonsense." He said it with a bit of heat, it must be admitted, because her lack of respect for the sacred was the worst he had ever heard. "What has my training got to do with the welfare state? The welfare state takes away from the head of the family his God-given right and duty to provide for those in his—"

"The welfare state takes care of those who can't take care of themselves, *when* they can't take care of themselves," she interrupted vehemently. "And that includes all of us at one time or another in our lives. Even yourself. And what's wrong with that, for Christ's sake? Aren't we all brothers and sisters in the human family? Didn't Christ say to love one another? So why shouldn't we look after each other?"

He was not about to be taken in by this Communist propaganda, even if it was disguised as Christian charity. "The welfare state," he said with an authority he felt the Irish bishops could be proud of, "is an instrument of future totalitarian aggression, and as such we must combat it at every turn. It does not propose to take care merely of the destitute but of all of us. As such it would destroy our freedom, make us dependent children of the omnipotent state, take away the authority of Holy Mother Church, destroy—"

"Will you listen to yourself!" she shouted. The dress went up, the legs uncrossed, and a pair of bare, parted knees thrust towards him from the sofa. "Your totalitarian church is afraid of a totalitarian state because the totalitarian state has got a bigger army than you have. But all you both want is to control us, the people. So we, the people, must get rid of both of you. Regardless of what you may have heard, Maura Higgins is no Communist. Democratic socialism is what this country needs.

And of course separation of church and state to go with it. Would you like a cup of tea?" And she was on her way to the kitchen before he could refuse.

She was gone a long time, leaving him sitting there all by himself. He could hear the hard clack of delft and cutlery and herself singing softly, as if she were happy about something. And he was trying to focus his mind on the right arguments to use against this wild woman and her Communist ideas and her hatred of Holy Mother Church. But he was being distracted by images of bare white legs and a rising dress and bare white arms. He hadn't been aware before that women grew hair under their arms and on their legs. Or was Maura Higgins an aberration in this as well as in her beliefs? Then she was back with a huge tray that had a silver teapot and china cups and saucers and a small plate of currant cake. "You can't have a good argument without the cup of tea," she said cheerfully, pouring and stirring and handing to him.

He didn't know what to say to that. He wasn't arguing for argument's sake, for God's sake, but to return this lost sheep to Christ, the Good Shepherd. And here she was treating his sacred ministry as if it were nothing more than a school debate. "They say you don't go to mass," he said, not looking at her, taking a bite out of the currant cake.

"Do they now?" But she said no more. She poured some milk in her own tea and stirred it. Then with the cup and saucer in one hand, she raised her legs and tucked them up under her on the sofa and draped the dress over them with the other hand. He had never seen a woman sit like that before.

"They say you don't believe in the Church anymore either," he persisted, feeling just a touch of satisfaction at having maneuvered the conversation to where he wanted it.

She sipped her tea and stirred it a little more, as if it weren't quite sweet enough. Then she looked up at him with the kind of half-amused tolerance that a mother would show to a child asking where the hen got the egg from. "What I believe," she said calmly, almost indulgently, "is a very personal matter between me and my God. So *they,* whoever they are, would do better to mind their own bloody business. And you can tell them that from me." She sipped daintily again, with the little finger raised. "Ah! There's nothing like the cup of tea." And she actually smiled at him.

For reasons he could never properly explain afterward, that smile caused the anger to rise swiftly inside him. There was this levity in her attitude, this facility for flipping suddenly from profound debate to a discussion of tea. She was making fun of him, was what it was, and through him of Holy Mother Church herself. "I don't think you take any of this in the least bit seriously," he said, and he could feel the acrimony in his own voice.

She didn't seem the least bothered by his annoyance, just kept looking straight at him. "I take my tea very seriously," she said quietly. "And I take my beliefs even more seriously." This almost in a whisper. "What I don't take seriously," her voice rising gradually like a wind out of the west before a winter storm, "is people *telling* me what I am to believe. I believe what I believe, just as you believe what you believe. And that's a phenomenon of nature, not something we have any control over. So if you want a fruitful discussion of the welfare state, I would advise you to stay away from any talk about Maura Higgins's religious beliefs and practices." And then she smiled at him again, but only with her lips this time. "Now, what were we talking about at all?"

He could feel the blood flow through his neck and the flush wash over his cheeks. The unmitigated gall of her! This layperson! This apostate Catholic! This spiritual felon from whose mouth came blasphemies! Telling *him* what he could or could not talk about! "We're talking about the state of your immortal soul, that's what we're talking about!" He was almost shouting. "About your not going to mass, about your hating the Church, about your disrespect for the pope himself, not to mention St. Paul. Good God Almighty!" He put down his tea as if it were poison to his soul and leaned forward in his chair. "Who do you think you are, woman? Isn't there anything sacred to you at all? Jesus Christ! I heard all those things about you, and I didn't believe them. I didn't want to believe them. But I do now. My advice to you, Mrs. Higgins, is to get on your bended knees right this very minute and beg forgiveness from Almighty God before He strikes you dead for your blasphemies. And then take yourself back to confession as quick as you can and spend the next six months in prayer before the Blessed Sacrament to make reparation for what you've said and done. And that's my advice to you." He ended weakly because at that very minute he looked up to see her reaction and found himself looking into soft brown eyes that were as warm as the summer sun.

"It's a terrible pity," Maura Higgins said. She wasn't

smiling, mind you. Or looking angry. Instead there was a great sadness in her face.

"What do you mean?" The words choked in his throat: he was feeling foolish already for his outburst, and now he didn't know what to make of her unnatural reaction to it.

"You're such a good-looking boy," she said. "You'd make a great coort for some girl. If I was single myself. . . . And you'd be a powerful preacher for the cause of socialism. Do you have to throw it all away on being a priest?"

She said it in such a sincere, almost reverend tone that the full force of the words didn't immediately strike him. Of course at that precise moment, it must be recorded, Phelim O'Brien, religious scholastic and tonsured cleric in minor orders, became suddenly and, in the circumstances, inexplicably mesmerized by the woman sipping tea on the sofa. It was totally out of his power not to be. When Maura Higgins put on the charm, you could never stay mad at her. If you were half a man at all you would want desperately for her to think well of you. And if you were a professional celibate you wouldn't even know what was happening to you. Poor Phelim hadn't the time to analyze what it was that washed over him like high tide on Galway Bay. Not since Catherine McGrath almost seduced him had he looked head on, as it were, into the eyes of an attractive woman. Daily, diligently, he practiced custody of the senses that he might not witness anything unbecoming or untoward to his priestly soul. Ankles and calves, unfortunately, and even occasional knees could not always be shut out when he was home on holidays, but these, with the help of prayer and mortification, the young cleric had learned to cope with fairly well. He had, however, no recent practice at all in what to do when directly confronted with a pair of eyes as entrancing as Maura Higgins's. "Jesus!" instantly sibilated capriciously from his anguished soul like a belch in the wake of a bicarbonate of soda. It was an ejaculatory prayer, it was the Lord's name in vain, it was the cri de coeur of a latent lecher as well as an agonized scream of total confusion and frustration, all rolled into one. "O, God!" he added, out of breath, as if not only the Son but the entire Trinity had to be invoked at that very minute against this sudden calamitous threat to his chastity.

"What's the matter?" Maura Higgins asked, instantly all innocent concern. "Are you feeling all right?" The legs swung off the sofa, revealing luscious tracts of soft white skin, and the flap of the dress dropped down to expose deep white bosom as she leaned forward solicitously to examine his condition. "Was it the tea? Maybe I made it too strong. I like the tea strong myself, mind you, but it doesn't agree with everybody."

"I . . ." Phelim began, not knowing what he was going to say next. Then of a sudden it hit his brain, like a football on the back of the head, what had just happened to him. He leaped out of the armchair, did a neat sideways step to avoid those advancing knees, backed hard into the piano, and then created great cacophonous chords as he leaned on the keys to project himself forward to the open door. Having established a proper distance and a safe escape route, he turned to face the cause of his turmoil. "Get thee behind me, Satan!" he roared. "Do not tempt the anointed of the Lord." He had to stop at that point because he was badly out of breath. Maura sat watching him from the couch without a stir out of her. "I am God's celibate, and you are trying to seduce me, Mrs. Higgins," he shouted. "May the Lord forgive you for that as well as for everything else you have done." Then he walked out the front door with all the bravura of a seasoned parish priest.

To give Maura Higgins her due, she never told anyone about the incident. Except for Eileen Maille, of course; she had to tell Eileen or she'd blow a gasket. But when they stopped laughing she did suggest to her friend that it would be in the best interest of the foolish young cleric if the story didn't go any further. So Eileen was careful not to talk about it, except to her fiancé, Timmy Mulligan. Timmy, between whom and Phelim there never had been any love lost and who moreover hated the living sight of Maura Higgins, gave a hilarious and somewhat bawdy rendition of the story, replete with much poetic license, to the patrons of his pub that night. Within a week a dozen different versions of the incident were circulating around Creevagh parish. The one that Mary Hughes was told by Mrs. McTigue in a shocked undertone after Tuesday morning mass was milder than some that were going around. But it was scabrous enough to warrant bringing the matter to the parish priest's attention. Which Mary Hughes dutifully did when she brought him his breakfast that very morning.

That same evening Father Coyne drove the Baby Ford back to Knockard. He met Phelim walking up the road saying his breviary. "There's a story going around about you," he said, having gotten out of the car and walking alongside his young protégé, hands behind his back. "I'd like to hear from your own lips that it is not true."

"A story!" said Phelim. In all innocence, mind you; not a word of the rumors had reached his own ears. "What story?"

"They're saying," said Father Coyne, looking down at his shiny black shoes, "and mind you, I don't believe them myself, but they're saying that you went back to Jack Higgins's house to exorcise the devil out of Jack's wife."

"I did no—" Phelim began, but Father Coyne continued.

"Now, while that might not be a bad thing in itself, given the recent behavior of Mrs. Higgins, it is a sacred function that is reserved to the parish priest to perform at his discretion. However, that's neither here nor there for the moment. What is most disturbing to me is that they're saying you first removed all your garments and then had the woman remove hers before you started the ritual. Now tell me straight, Phelim, that it isn't true, and I'll believe you, and we'll say no more on the subject."

Father Coyne stopped and turned and looked Phelim O'Brien right in the eye. The parish priest's was a wicked eye indeed, and one under which strong farmers remiss in their Easter duty had been known to quail. But Phelim O'Brien was a veteran of seven years in the scholasticate, where mentors were chosen as much for severity as for pious wisdom, and he did not flinch. "That is a black lie," he said, the anger rising quickly in him at the enormity of the accusation. "I only went back to talk her out of her Communist beliefs. What kind of people are they at all who invent such calumnies?" His arms shot heavenward in dramatic appeal to the Almighty. The breviary flew from his right hand and landed on the grassy margin. He picked it up and wiped it off and stood shaking his head in disbelief at the awful perversity of mankind.

"You need say no more," Father Coyne said. "I believe you entirely. People tend to exaggerate things a bit." And he immediately went on to talk about the weather, which had been warm and sunny for several days now, though mind you it looked like rain this evening.

But people often remember lies far longer than truth. The wild fiction of Phelim's bawdy exorcism entered the folklore of Creevagh parish and is still occasionally recalled with relish by a besotted patron of Paddy Gannon's pub.

The

Communist

Threat

Preparations

for

a

Wedding

F RANCIE Madden was back at the Kilmolara railway
station doing a bit of business with the fireman on
the Dublin train when he spotted Jack Mulligan
getting off. What kind of business it was that Francie
himself was after he didn't tell the patrons of Gannon's
that night when he mentioned nonchalantly that the
black sheep of the Mulligan clan had returned. And no
one thought to ask him in the buzz of conversation his
news aroused.

"He's home for the wedding," Pat Moloney pronounced astutely.

"Why wouldn't he?" Paddy Gannon agreed. "All the

money in South Mayo will be there. Maybe he thinks he'll be able to get his hands on some of it."

"Or on some of the ladies that'll be there," Jimmy Mc-Tigue said sourly. Jack had once tried to court Jimmy's own daughter, Annie May, before she ran away with Philpot Emmet, but Jimmy had sent him packing with the forceful threat of a boot in the arse.

"You think now he'd be ashamed to be seen here after what he did," said Johnny Lydon, himself a pillar of rectitude in dealings with the opposite sex.

"The lads will be glad to have him for the match against Kilmolara on Sunday," Thomas Ruane noted. "He's a great kicker entirely."

Jack Mulligan, the subject of their discussion, was the brother of Timmy Mulligan, the prosperous owner of Mulligan's Bar, Victuals, and Grocery and soon to be the happy bridegroom of Eileen Maille, the beauty of Turloughmor. To be more precise, Jack was the oldest of Timmy's three younger brothers. After him came Michael, who had married into a well-to-do publican's family in Castlebar two years ago, and Matty, who, though not particularly gifted with brains, was a fierce hard worker and had managed to get himself qualified as a doctor and was now practicing medicine up in Galway just outside Oranmore. In the matter of brains, by a rather peculiar quirk of nature most of the gray matter passed along by old Martin to his children had gone to Jack, the one who was least inclined to use it and who had, as a matter of fact, squandered it completely. One of the brainiest scholars he had ever had, outside of Phelim O'Brien, but a complete wastrel nevertheless, was how Addis Emmet once described him, adding something to the effect of what else could you expect from such a family. The Creevagh schoolmaster held his grudge against the entire Mulligan clan.

Anyway, Jack went to University College, Galway to become a veterinarian because his father made him go. But divil a bit of studying he did there, though it was said he did more than his share of late-night carousing. And after two years they threw him out of the university for what in the letter sent home to his father they termed "licentious behavior," even though he was a great asset to the college Gaelic football team. He came home then and spent his time kicking football, at which he was very good, and chasing the girls, at which he was very good too, until he got one of them into a family way and had to go to England in a hurry while Martin Mulligan's influence and money arranged for a discreet birth and orphanage placement. Jack had not set foot in the parish since then, not even when his father died, and it was assumed that Creevagh had happily seen the last of him.

Of course, the principal item of conversation in Gannon's and in all of Creevagh at this time was the wedding itself. Everyone who was anyone, and a lot who weren't, were invited. Timmy, an even shrewder businessman than his father, left no one out who had ever been or who might one day be a customer. He was renting a tent from Galway, he said, that would cover half the field at the back of his house where the Creevagh team played its football matches. And that's where the reception was going to be, he said, over the objections of his mother, who thought that the Ardilaun House in Taylor's Hill up in Galway would be a more appropriate and genteel place for such a grand occasion. Part of the tent would have a wooden floor so there could be dancing. And to provide music Timmy was hiring his favorite dance band, Mairtin Heaney and his Glen Miller Sound, all the way from Claremorris. A haberdasher from Kilmolara was hired to decorate the entire inside of the tent with fancy hangings and streamers. As for food, Peter Solon had been told to butcher a bullock and six sheep for the occasion. And two fellows came up from Castlebar to build big spits in the back yard on which the animals were going to be roasted. Ten local ladies were being hired to help prepare the food and serve it. And when it came to booze, well, half a lorryload of half barrels of Guinness had already been delivered as well as lashings of Irish whiskey for the serious drinkers and minerals of all kinds for the members of the Pioneer Total Abstinence Association. Altogether, it was going to be the biggest bash that the parish of Creevagh had ever seen.

Eileen Maille, the bride-to-be, was in two minds about the whole business. Of course, she had been in two minds about Timmy Mulligan ever since she had promised to marry him last year, and she still wasn't sure she was doing the right thing. Which was why she had made him set the wedding day a full year ahead when they became engaged. Even then, when Seamus Laffey came to her door last month and wished her a happy life and told her he was off to England in the morning, she broke down and cried. She had a real soft spot for Seamus, and when she saw him walking away down the boreen that evening with his arms swinging and he whistling to himself, she had half a mind to shout after him to come back and she'd marry him. But she didn't, and now she was committed to becoming Mrs. Timothy Mulligan, the richest woman, by virtue of her husband's wealth, in all of South Mayo. She'd have more clothes than any ten women in the parish, Timmy told her grandly, and he had already given her a power of money to buy some of them. But she had bought nothing yet, apart from having a fitting for the wedding dress. She was sitting in the kitchen one afternoon wondering what do with all that money that her mother said was ill gotten anyway, God help us, when Jack Mulligan suddenly turned up on her doorstep.

Mind you, she didn't know Jack well at all. The rake of Creevagh, who used to make it his business to court every good-looking girl in the parish, stayed very much away from her. That was because Timmy had informed him in no uncertain terms that if he so much as set his two eyes at the same time on Eileen Maille, by God he, Timothy Joseph Mulligan, would remake his, Jack Mulligan's, nose into an exact image and likeness of the Mulligan clan proboscis. Now it was a remarkable fact that although three of the four brothers were plagued with the great tom turkey beak of their father, Jack and his sister, Mona, had been gifted with the delightfully regular features and classically chiseled nose of the mother. So as a result of Jack Mulligan's pride in his facial structure, Eileen Maille until this moment had never gotten more than a distant hello from Martin Mulligan's prodigal son.

"To what do we owe the pleasure?" She had never stood this close to him in her life, and her first reaction there at her front door was a kind of tingling that went straight from the top of her head all the way down to her bare feet. To give Jack his due, and not to mind all the envious bad mouthing that was done about him, he was a fine cut of a man with his black hair and big shoulders. And he had a kind of a presence about him that few women could resist.

"The boss sent me back with some sausages for your mother; they came in fresh from Castlebar this morning." He had a deep, mellifluous voice, and there was a sort of pleased surprise in his dark, wide eyes that made Eileen feel she was the most beautiful woman he had ever seen.

"Come in," she said. "My mother is down the field looking at a sick calf." She noticed with surprise Timmy's motorcar by the front gate. Her husband-to-be never let anyone drive his V8.

"They tell me you're going to marry himself," he remarked, handing over the sausages that were carefully wrapped in brown paper.

"I suppose I am." But, for some reason she didn't understand, she felt terribly embarrassed at having to admit that fact to this extremely handsome younger brother.

"Well, that's great now. 'Tis a good thing that some of us are able to find the right woman and settle down. I've never been lucky in that department myself." And he flashed a kind of shy grin that forced Eileen Maille to stand on one bare foot, as if the floor beneath her were too hot to stand on.

"Would you like a cup of tea?" Never in all her born days had she appreciated more the virtues of that extraordinary potation. Never mind the Guinness; it was the tea that was the center of hospitality in every Irish house: it was the strengthening of ties among friends and neighbors, the breaking down of awkwardness with strangers, the excuse to prolong a visit by accepting or to cut one short by refusing. Jack Mulligan, who never drank the stuff if he could possibly help it, accepted now with alacrity, and the two of them sat and talked at the kitchen table until the mother came back from dosing her sick calf. Jack immediately got up, remembering all of a sudden that he had other things to do.

"Look what he brought you," Eileen said.

"Well, you're great entirely." Mrs. Maille had developed a taste for the sausages ever since Timmy started sending them over. The pity was she couldn't bring herself to like Timmy himself as much. "Arrah, what's your hurry?" she said now to Jack, also feeling a bit of nature for this young man who everyone said was a rogue. "Have another cup of tea." So Jack stayed a bit longer and drank more tea. And then Eileen's brother Joe came in from the bog and supper was laid on the table and Jack was persuaded to join in the meal. And he sat afterwards by the fire with them and in response to their questions told them what life was like in London. And he talked about the greatest shop in the world, Harrods, where he had worked as a clerk for a time before he got tired of standing around in a suit all day smiling at people. He was working for a shipping company now, making good money, mind you, but he'd rather come home and live in Dublin, which was what he was planning to do in the near future.

And all the while Eileen couldn't keep her eyes off him. He was easy to watch because after the mother came in he paid all his attention to Mrs. Maille and then later on to Joe, hardly ever looking in her direction at all. She didn't know what had gotten into her, staring at him like that, and as a matter of fact she didn't care either. As

soon as he left, after shaking hands with everyone including herself and saying what a wonderful time he had
had and promising to come back to see them soon again
now that he was about to become a brother-in-law, she
went straight back to her room and lay on the bed. Her
head was spinning. Her mind was numb. Her whole
body was tingling the way it would after you came in
from the cold and spent a few minutes standing in front
of a warm fire.

He was back again a few evenings later, this time on a
bicycle. An evening when Timmy was not expected. The
fiancé was very regular in his visiting habits, you see:
Tuesdays, Thursdays, Saturdays, and Sundays only. Jack
came to see Joe, he said, and talk a bit about the football
match with Ballindine that was coming up, Joe being
captain of the Creevagh team since Seamus Laffey's departure. And he went off down the yard to find her
brother despite Eileen's invitation to come in and have a
cup of tea and wait for him there. Later he and Joe came
up to the house and sat in the kitchen talking football
until supper. And Joe asked Jack to stay for a bite to eat,
and Jack did. And he stayed on after till ten o'clock. And
then he knelt for the rosary with them, even saying the
fourth decade in a smooth, even rhythmic tone on invitation from Mrs. Maille.

But during the entire evening he hardly looked at
Eileen except when politeness demanded. Needless to
say, she was dying. Part of her was singing like a bird,
thrilled to be near him and to be able to look at him,
though she was very discreet about it. The other part of
her was both baffled and piqued. Ever since she was a girl
she was accustomed to the lads taking *too* much notice

of her, and she had developed a kind of cool reserve for coping with that, especially since she hadn't much interest in most of them. Now here was someone whose attention she wanted and all he was doing was talking about football with her brother. She would have been mad at him except that he gave her a big smile and a warm goodnight when he was leaving. Later, back in her room, she came to the startling conclusion that his ignoring her was just a game he was playing: pretending not to notice her so she'd pay attention to him. He'd know about her reputation for being aloof: Maura Higgins often told her the lads were saying she was stuck up. Anyway, that thought made her feel better. She fell asleep thinking about his smile and the shape of his shoulders and the wave of his hand as he walked out the door.

The next evening when Timmy came back he wanted to know if she had bought her new wardrobe. They were going someplace very elegant for the honeymoon, he said, though he wouldn't say where—that was to be a surprise. But she'd need to be dressed up a lot and he couldn't understand, he said, and he seemed a bit annoyed too, by the look of him, when she told him she hadn't done any shopping yet. "There isn't much to be got in Kilmolara anyway," she said by way of excuse.

"I'll take you up to Galway tomorrow, then, and we'll get everything you need." Timmy was very decisive when it came to getting things done. But the next morning it was the younger brother, not Timmy, who came to get her in the V8.

"He had to go to Castlebar himself in the lorry to see about some business," Jack explained casually. Eileen put on a face as if she were displeased, but of course she was delighted. Jack looked so handsome, dressed in his Sunday best and with a watch chain hanging out of his vest pocket. Then she felt guilty about preferring the brother to her fiancé. Then she didn't know what to think when all the way up to Galway he hardly spoke to her except in answer to something she'd say. This was carrying the hard-to-get game a bit too far. Only once did he talk spontaneously about anything, and that was when they passed a long, high brick wall in the midst of which were set a pair of huge, rusty iron gates hanging listlessly open.

"That place belonged to an old landlord," he said. "I've been reading about them lads in a history book lately. I read a lot, you know." He was staring straight ahead at the road with a very serious expression on his face. "It was a terrible state of affairs for the poor farmers back in those days. All this land for miles around belonged to the landlord, and the tenants could stay on it only at his pleasure. And they had to pay him high rents for the privilege and take off their hats whenever they met him." He glanced sideways with a sort of bleak grin, the first time he had looked at her since they left Turloughmor. "Of course some of us still aren't much better off."

"And what does that mean?" Eileen said it a bit tartly; she was feeling piqued at him by now. "Every farmer owns his land these days. Ever since the Wyndham Act," she added, just to show him she knew her Irish history quite well, thank you.

"I was thinking about myself," he said. "I'm living at home, and I have a job only at my brother's pleasure."

"I thought you had a job in London." There was something odd about the way he was talking.

"I'm home to stay," he said. "Working for Timmy.

England is a terrible place altogether. You wouldn't get me going back there again." He said this with great vehemence, and then he said nothing more till they reached Galway and parked the V8 in Eyre Square. "I'll meet you here at five," he said after he took the gold watch out of his vest pocket and looked at it.

"Aren't you going to stay with me? I'll need someone to help with the packages." She was still looking forward to spending the afternoon with him, despite his silence on the way up. A bit of lunch in Lydon's would thaw him out and she'd have him eating out of her hand in no time, was what she was thinking.

"I have a few things to do, a few fellows I have to see." He was looking across the square at the Great Southern Hotel instead of at her, a fact that annoyed Eileen no end. "You can put the packages in the boot." And his face assumed some kind of a cross between a grin and a grimace. "Your fiancé cleaned it out especially for you this morning," he added.

"It's locked," she said crossly; she was beginning to get mad at him. Beautiful Eileen Maille was not accustomed to lads treating her in this offhand fashion.

"I'll give you the key," he said. And he did. And then he walked off in the direction of the Great Southern without another word.

Eileen was livid. But she calmed down as soon as she got into a dress shop. She bought a few things and took them back to Eyre Square and put them in the boot of the car. Then she went to Lydon's for lunch and felt a lot better. She was still mad at Jack, but then she would think of those dreamy eyes and want not to be. It was hard on the creature to have to come back home and work for Timmy. England must be a terrible place to live in. She had heard stories about it, which was why she would never go there herself. And which, when you came down to it, was most likely why she was marrying Timmy Mulligan instead of Seamus Laffey. In the afternoon she visited every shop that looked the least bit promising, and by five o'clock the boot was full of parcels, though she still had half the money Timmy had given her. She was feeling warm, even a little sweaty, for it was a very mild late August afternoon.

She had to wait ten minutes, sitting in the car, before Jack turned up. But the annoyance that was building up in her again evaporated the minute he appeared and smiled at her through the window. He opened the driver's door and stuck his head in. "Where's all the clothes?" She caught a whiff of whiskey.

"They're in the boot, where else?"

He was staring at her. "You should have them on you." Again that dreamy look in his eyes. "I'd like to see you wearing what you bought."

"They're for the honeymoon." He had had too much to drink was what she was thinking.

"Put something on for me now," he pleaded, very softly, looking straight at her. "I'd like to see you all dressed up."

"Go on out of that." She waved him away. "Don't be foolish."

"I'd be terribly obliged if you would." He didn't move, and those big dark eyes of his would melt ice off the North Pole.

"Where would I change?" Mind you, the same thought had occurred to Eileen herself earlier on; she wouldn't mind at all arriving home dressed up in some of her new finery. "I'm not about to take my clothes off here in the car."

"No, no! Of course not." Not so much as a smile out of him. "You can change at the Great Southern. There's a ladies' room just down from the bar. I'll show you where it is."

"Don't be daft," she said.

"Go on," he argued.

"You're stark raving mad," she said. But she went anyway, taking several parcels from the boot. Humor them when they're drunk, her mother always said. When she came out of the ladies' room, dressed in a bright yellow frock and nylon stockings and white high-heeled shoes and a small white hat with lace on it, he was nowhere to be seen. She walked up past the bar looking for him, and then she heard the voice from behind saying, "Don't you look gorgeous." And he held her arm lightly all the way back to Eyre Square. In the car she could smell the whiskey again and wished he could have been a Pioneer like Seamus Laffey. When they were out on the Headford road she asked him what he had done all day, just to make conversation.

"I went to see a man about a dog." Again that crooked mixture of grin and grimace. "I know a lot of lads here from my days at the uni." And then he lapsed back into silence.

It was beginning to get dark when they came by the old brick-walled demesne. He slowed down, then without warning pulled the car in by the gate and stopped. "I want to show you something." He got out, walked 'round the car, and opened her door.

"Isn't it a bit late? I'd like to get home."

"It'll only take a minute," he said. So she got out and followed him through the gate and along an overgrown path between tall bushes. She had to pick her steps carefully; it wasn't easy to walk with high heels on the thick-grassed, uneven ground. "We're almost there," he said several times. Then they came around a bend in the path, and there just ahead was the silhouette of a roofless old mansion, its chimneys tall and stark against the pale light of the late evening sky.

"Is this what you brought me to see?" Her feet were beginning to hurt in the new shoes.

"Come on in," he said. "I want to show you something." He led the way through a gaping hole that had once been a doorway and stopped inside on a patch of grass. "This was the great hall of Lord Kilmaine's mansion," he said, waving his arm in a sweeping half circle. "From here he ruled over his tenants and decided their fate: whether they could stay or whether they had to go; what he would take from them and what he would leave to them." He rubbed his hands together in the satisfied manner of Mr. Addis Emmet. "It must have been a great feeling of power."

"I'm sure it was," Eileen said. "Now let us go home." He reminded her of her father, the Lord have mercy on him, the way he would come in from Gannon's of a night half drunk and spout pretentious nonsense about everything and anything.

"Did you know," he said, craning his neck to look up at a chimney, "that Lord Kilmaine used to exercise his droit du seigneur here when his tenants got married?"

"His what?" She was beginning to worry if he'd be able to drive the rest of the way home.

"Droit du seigneur. First-night rights on every bride.

Cripes!" He put his head back and shrieked like a banshee. "That old bugger had more fun than a tomcat in a barnful of pussies."

"And you're as drunk as a lord, Jack Mulligan," Eileen said. "Take me home now." She turned to walk back out, but he grabbed her arm and held on tightly so she couldn't move away. "Let me go," she yelled, suddenly annoyed, pulling to free herself. "What in God's name do you think you're doing?"

"I love you, Eileen." He jerked her towards him. "I have always loved you, but Timmy wouldn't let me." His face was close and the whiskey breath strong.

"You're drunk, Jack. Now let me go." She pulled again, but his grip just tightened the more.

"Maybe I am," he said. "But I know what I want. And what I want right now is my droit du seigneur." And he said it with such desperate urgency as to scare the living daylights out of Eileen Maille.

"Jack Mulligan," she screamed, "if you don't let my arm go this very second I'll tell Timmy that you misbehaved, and then you won't have a job in Creevagh either."

"Fook bleddy Timmy! He's the reason I never got my hands on you before." He grabbed her other arm and pulled her very close. The whiskey smell was awful. She kicked at his shins, but he paid no heed. "Do you know that I've been mad about you for years? But he said he'd kill me stone dead if I ever touched you." She tried a knee to the groin, but he sidestepped without letting go. 'Stay away from her,' the bloody bastard was always saying, 'she's mine.' Well, right now you're mine." And he pulled her tightly to him with those fierce, strong arms of his. "I'd like to see the bugger's face on the wedding night when he finds that Jack has been there first."

"Let me go," she screamed again, tugging desperately, digging her high heels into the grass. And then he did, suddenly, pushing her away from him. And just as quickly lurched to what had been the entrance when this ruin was a mansion. Eileen looked around for another way out, but the two arched doorways that led from this once great hall were now blocked with great piles of stones. "Jack!" She held up her hands to ward him off. "Don't be foolish, now. Let me go, there's a good lad, and we'll say nothing more about it. I won't tell Timmy on you."

"Take your frock off so it won't get ruined on the grass." He was still standing in the gap, breathing hard, bending slightly, legs apart, hands on hips, like a goalie waiting for a penalty shot.

"Don't be daft, Jack. Look! I'll give you a kiss when we get back to the car. All right?" The terror was beginning to make her knees feel weak.

"Take everything off." It hit her ear like the bellow of a bull at the sight of a cow. "I'll do the same." And he struggled out of jacket and trousers and underpants, all the time keeping an eye on her. And then he stood there in the gap with his shirt tails only half covering his nakedness. "Come on," he said, coaxing, crouching, arms waving, moving slowly towards her like a farmer trying to corner a recalcitrant sheep with the maggots. "There's a good girl, now. Easy does it." And he made a sudden grab that she barely avoided and at the cost of losing one of her high heels.

"Stop it, Jack!" she screamed. "You'll be sorry for

Preparations

for

a

Wedding

165

this." He was forcing her into a corner, and it was hard to move with only the one shoe on. She bent quickly and pulled it off.

"Gently, polly. Gently." He was almost cooing. Then he lunged again, arms outstretched. This time she could not sidestep. Instinctively her arms shot up in self-protection. The heel of the shoe in her right hand came in crunching contact with his face, and it was Jack Mulligan's turn to scream. She saw the blood spurt from his nose for a brief second before she dodged around him and ran for the gap. The years of running barefoot through the fields as a nipper stood her in good stead. She reached the road and the car before she dared look back. He was nowhere in sight. She kept on going as if she would run all the way home to Creevagh, feeling the friction of tarmacadam on her soles through the thin nylon stockings. She was out of breath, but her legs kept moving. And her eyes kept searching through the half darkness for a house that she could run to. Then, when she was exhausted, there was the sound of the car from behind. She scrambled over the fragile wall, ignoring the falling stones and her ripping frock. On her knees, crouching, peering through the spaces, she watched him pass slowly in the dim light. He had a handkerchief to his face and his head was swiveling every which way. Then he was gone and she lay prone beneath the wall, shivering, suddenly cold all over.

She lay there for a long time, her eyes fixed on a bright star that shone through the still-light sky. Venus, the evening star, Seamus Laffey had once told her. A great man for the stars, Seamus. The soles of her feet were stinging. Her arms ached where Jack the madman had held them too tightly. Her lungs still hurt from too much unaccustomed running. And her mind was numb from the fear that had paralyzed it.

But then something began to happen. Maybe it came from that white, unblinking star of love. She was staring at it, wishing to God she had never set eyes on Jack Mulligan, when deep inside her the warming started. It began slowly, like the effect of hot tea when you came in out of a winter night. Then it spread and spread till it covered her entire body, and suddenly she was boiling all over with an anger that was trying to burst out of her skin. She jumped up suddenly and grabbed a stone and climbed back over the wall and stood at the side of the road in the three-quarter darkness, ready to smash his bloody face in if he so much as came near her. It was then that she heard the car in the distance again. He was coming back. For a moment the fear returned, but she stood her ground, the stone held tightly in both hands, not caring that her ripped frock was hanging off her shoulder. She would kill him stone dead the minute he came near enough.

The car slowed, passed, then stopped and reversed. She had to scramble back up the bank to avoid being hit. It stopped again and the door opened. She raised the stone above her head, then lost her balance and slid down the bank, bumping into the bonnet. And all her energy evaporated with the force of the collision. He'd get her for sure now, was what went through her mind.

"Good God, woman, what are you doing at all?" It sounded awfully like Father Coyne's voice.

"It's Eileen Maille," she said, not moving, not able to straighten her body, half thinking she was only dreaming and that Jack Mulligan would start pulling her clothes off any minute. But she was too tired now to resist.

"Eileen! Is it Eileen? Eileen Maille?" The priest sounded totally bewildered. "Are you all right? Are you hurt? How in God's name did you get here?" The questions just tumbled out.

"Can I get into the car, Father? I'm cold." Then the floodgates opened and Eileen Maille started bawling. She leaned over, both hands on the bonnet, and shook and blubbered and sobbed, her head lying limp, her hair hanging down and tearing sounds coming out of her throat that would match the wails of the damned. Father Coyne, the poor man, just stood there and watched. Not a word did he utter until the heaving slowed down and the shivering stopped and Eileen Maille was able to stand up straight and say, "Sorry, Father. I'm terribly sorry, but I'm awfully upset."

"Why don't you get in, now?" the priest said. "We can talk on the way home." And she did. And they did. He asked the questions and she forced some kind of answers out of her mouth. The last thing in the world she wanted now was talk, but you didn't say no to Father Coyne. He wanted details. Did the blackguard touch her? Did he kiss her? Was she sure he didn't? How did she provoke him in the first place? What kind of encouragement had she given him? She felt herself getting sick, and then she vomited on the floor of the car, barely missing her yellow dress and stockinged feet.

"Well, thanks be to God nothing happened," Father Coyne pronounced after he finished his examination, his eyes steady on the dark road ahead. "You are still virgo intacta. A virgin," he explained. Then he added soothingly, "You'll feel better in the morning."

That started the bawling again, but she quickly stifled it and just sobbed quietly for the rest of the journey. At the house she dried her eyes with her fingers and thanked Father Coyne and said yes, it might be better if he didn't come in. But she didn't respond at all to his parting admonition that she come back to confession as soon as possible.

Jack Mulligan was never seen in Creevagh again. Timmy's car was found near the Kilmolara railway station next day, and Timmy in a great rage came roaring back in it to the Maille house looking for an explanation. "What in bloody hell's name happened yesterday?" By way of greeting, the moment Eileen opened the front door.

"Your fecking brother is going to jail for what he did," she cannoned back at him, without so much as letting him inside.

Now, a lesser man would have stopped right there, properly intimidated by the fire coming out of her eyes and the smoke from her nostrils. But not Timmy Mulligan. "What went on between you two?" he bellowed.

"I don't need this," Eileen screamed and slammed the door in his face.

But he was around to the back and into the kitchen before she had time to start crying. "What in God's name happened?" Still shouting, even with the mother standing at the table making bread.

"Your brother tried to ravish my daughter," Mrs. Maille said. "That's what happened." Very calmly, not looking up and not interrupting the rhythm of her kneading.

"I hate him!" Eileen screamed. "I hate you all. You're

no good, any damn one of you. Go to hell! Leave me alone! I never want to see you again." And she turned and raced back to her room and slammed that door too.

The screaming had a calming effect on Timmy. He sat down by the fire and stared into the hot coals for a while. Mrs. Maille continued her kneading. "He's a terrible scoundrel entirely," Timmy said eventually.

"I would flog him within an inch of his life if he was here this minute," Mrs. Maille said, suddenly pounding the dough with great viciousness. "He's a low cur dog, so he is."

"How can I make it up to her?" Timmy was a terribly practical man.

"Leave her be," the mother said. "She has to get over it in her own time."

For once in his life Timmy took advice from a woman. He stayed away for a whole week, with the preparations still going on, mind you, and the wedding only another week away. And when on Sunday afternoon he went back to see her he took with him a tiny puppy dog, a poodle he had bought up in Galway for a terrible sum of money. Mrs. Maille saw him coming and met him at the front door.

"She's gone," she said without letting him in. "Up to Dublin. Staying with a cousin of her father. She said to tell you if you want a wedding not to wait for her." And Mrs. Maille, known to be one of the nicest people in Creevagh parish, slammed the door hard in Timmy Mulligan's face.

Philpot
the
Repentant

THREE years and three months to the day after Philpot Emmet "eloped," he and Annie May returned to Creevagh. They came just a week before Christmas, the Monday of the Margadh Mor in Kilmolara, when every farmer's wife who had reared a turkey or a goose was down in Main Street trying to flog the bird for a pound or two so she could buy some Christmas things for the children.

Thomas Ruane it was that first spotted the happy family's return. He was coming home a bit late from town, having cajoled a couple of shillings out of his sister Maggie after she sold a turkey and two geese so he could wet his whistle before undertaking the long walk back to Kildotia. With the makings of a last pint still in his pocket as he came up the road towards Paddy Gannon's, he told himself he'd keep it there until Saturday night. But a man's plans are subject to change when warranted by events. He was passing the graveyard, and it just beginning to get dark, when the sound of the motorcar came from behind. He stood at the entrance to God's own acre and glanced into the interior of Mike Carney's hackney as it passed. Thomas had great eyesight, and as he told the patrons of Gannon's later that same night, he'd recognize the shape of Philpot's head anywhere.

"Men!" said Paddy Gannon in the high-pitched voice he used for formal pronouncements. "Let ye lock up your wives and daughters tonight; the wild bull of Creevagh is loose among us once more."

"There was a woman holding a babby in the car too, on my oath," Thomas Ruane added.

"You don't say!" said Pat Moloney. "Annie May, no doubt about it. Himself is not here tonight, and he's always here on a Monday." Himself being Jimmy McTigue, Annie May's father, who in the more than three years since his daughter's departure had never once mentioned her name.

It was indeed Annie May that Thomas saw. And the child she held was none other than Alphonsus James Emmet, the fruit of her passionate union with Philpot and, according to the bad-minded gossips of the parish, the cause of their hasty departure in the first place. Be that as it may, they were back. And staying with Mr. and Mrs. Emmet in the schoolmaster's residence. And on Christmas morning not only attending mass—thereby causing some small amounts of money wagered in both Gannon's and Mulligan's drinking establishments to change hands—but even kneeling at the altar rails in the company of Addis and Mrs. to receive the Holy Eucharist. Since it was known that Philpot had not performed either his Christmas or Easter duty the year he ran away, this latter deed was the source of no minor amazement to close observers.

"Faith, 'tis a wonder Father Coyne gave him Communion at all," said Maggie Ruane on the way home that morning. "After all he's done."

"Well thanks be to God anyway," said Brigid Moloney. "He's made his peace with the Man Above."

"Maybe he has and maybe he hasn't," said Maggie, whose faith in the essential goodness of human nature was weaker than her friend's. "For myself, I wouldn't trust that lad as far as I could throw a bull by the horns."

But Philpot continued to astound with his newfound virtue. At the altar rails every Sunday in the company of Annie May and Mr. and Mrs. Addis. And down to visit Knock Shrine with Father Coyne not once but twice in the months after coming home. There were even stories that he planned to do St. Patrick's Purgatory in Lough Derg as soon as that place of severe penance opened up in the spring. "I'm a new man," he told Timmy Mulligan, who ran into him up in Galway. "The old wildness is gone, you see. 'Tis great what marriage and a family and the fear of God can do for a man. You settle down and you don't want to be running around anymore."

"It's a great institution indeed," said Timmy, still on the lookout himself for a suitable woman after being ditched last year by Eileen Maille. "And how is the house?" A touch of the patronizing in his tone; he had built a grand new home for himself since the father's death, whereas young Emmet had just moved into a modest cottage near Turloughmor that was recently vacated by a deceased widow.

"Ah, sure, it will do us fine," Philpot said humbly. "We're fortunate to have it at all, you know. God has been very good to us after what we've done to offend Him."

"You're back in the bank again, I hear," Timmy observed hurriedly. The unction in Philpot's tone was making him want to vomit.

"I am, thanks be to the Good God."

And to a lot of other people too, said Timmy to himself. It was known that a multitude of strings had been pulled to make it happen. By Addis and Father Coyne, of course. And Jack Higgins the county councilor. Even Timmy himself, who was a big customer of the bank, had been approached by Jack to put in a good word. And it was rumored that Tom Blowick, the T.D. for South Mayo, had been asked to intercede as well. In any event, within a month of his return from England Philpot was driving an old Morris Minor through the village of Creevagh at half eight every morning on his way up to the Bank of Ireland in Galway and returning home to Annie May and Alphonsus like clockwork every evening at half five. Paddy Gannon, standing at the door of his pub, would watch him pass and wonder what it was that had transformed the wild young Pisspot into this pious family man. "'Tis maybe in the blood after all," he said to himself, thinking of Addis and Mrs. But in his bones knowing there was more to it than met the eye. He was right about that.

The immediate cause of Philpot's absconding nearly three and a half years earlier had been Annie May's delicate state. He ran off to escape the consequences of his youthful lust. However, Annie May, propelled it was said by a kick in the arse from her father, quickly ran after the boyo and caught up with him in London. And Alphonsus arrived just six months later. Born, it must be conceded, outside the holy bonds of wedlock. Annie May was for getting married immediately, but Philpot demurred. "I no longer believe in the Roman Catholic Church," he declared defiantly, and that was that. But he did, to give him his due, provide support for his unfortunate sweetheart. He got himself a job in a bank and found them a tiny love nest out in Kilburn.

It was in that flat, with the help of Mrs. Nora Daly, a midwife from County Clare, and Mary Ellen McGee, their very good neighbor across the hall, that Alphonsus James was born. Having called Mary Ellen in a sweaty panic the evening that Annie May started showing signs of distress and waited in a state of nail-biting agitation until Nurse Daly arrived, Philpot adjourned to Mc-Sweeney's, the local Irish pub, to fortify himself for the outcome with the help of a few drafts of Guinness and a little Jameson.

He admitted afterwards to one of the lads in Mc-Sweeney's that he was less than enthusiastic at the first sight of his son. Arriving home after closing time, and considerably inebriated, as was only to be expected in the circumstances, he was presented by a stern-faced Nurse Daly with a tiny bundle wrapped in a blanket. Only from the neck up was the infant visible, but that alone was more than Philpot's delicate constitution could withstand. Red and wrinkled and hairless, the baby bore no resemblance whatever to the visage that Philpot admired in his morning mirror and which he had firmly expected would be replicated in this latest scion of the noble Emmet clan. He quickly returned the bundle to Mrs. Daly and retired to the tiny bathroom for a relieving bout of retching.

Annie May did not look much better when he was well enough to see her. The face streaked with sweat and the red hair he used to so admire looking like a rat's nest on the pillow made him want to turn and run the minute he saw her. She complained of weakness and pain, and after making her a cup of tea he was glad to adjourn to the couch in the tiny sitting room. That night, unable to sleep himself, what with having to listen to Annie May's moaning and the baby's crying, he swore on the blood of his great Emmet ancestors that never again would he be responsible for getting a woman in a family way. But time and food and nature their wonders did perform. It amazed him how fast Annie May recovered. And the infant lost his redness and his wrinkles and began, Philpot swore, to look the spitting image of himself. Almost overnight he turned into a proud father. His drinking friends from McSweeney's were constantly regaled with descriptions of this infant wonder, and several of them were dragged up to the flat to see for themselves.

A great crowd of blokes, the fellows who drank in McSweeney's. Philpot felt very much at home with them, particularly with a lad from Ballindine with whom he spent a lot of time discussing the fortunes and misfortunes of the Mayo football team. He was a bit unfortunate himself at times too: losing his job in the bank when some overzealous supervisor smelled a little whiskey on his breath one morning. And another time having to spend a night at the police station after he tried to break up a fight in McSweeney's between a couple of farm laborers from Tipperary. But he got back on his feet in no time at all, finding a job in the building trade as a plasterer with the help of a union card supplied by McSweeney himself and a few quick lessons on how to handle cement by the lad from Ballindine. The money was good in the building business, a lot more than he had been making in the wretched bank. And he handed over a reasonable amount of it to Annie May every week, which he fully expected would keep that young woman happy.

But Annie May wasn't happy. It would be gratifying to relate that the two and a half years since Alphonsus's birth were a time of bliss for her and her family; however, truth makes its own uncompromising demands. For one thing, Philpot drank too much. In the pub three and four nights a week and regular as clockwork coming home on Friday nights with the glazed look of the semi-drunk. Add to that his roving eye that was a constant source of worry. More than once he staggered up to the flat accompanied by a young woman who promptly fled on finding a rival glaring at her across the doorway. Then there were the occasions when he didn't come home at all. And the times that she found the lipstick on his handkerchiefs. Such an accumulation of facts might suggest some form of marital infidelity but for the fact that they weren't married. And this was what most stuck in Annie May's craw. She felt sure that if only she could get him to the altar and formally tie the knot, Philpot's drinking and carousing would cease and he would settle down to be a good husband and father. Besides, her conscience was nagging her for not going to mass or confession for the past two years. And about living in sin. And for not having Alphonsus baptized. Especially the latter. Finally, one morning when she could stand it no longer, she went down to the rectory after Philpot left for work. The housekeeper showed her into the parlor. "He needs to be baptized, Father," she told the priest, pointing to the little lad who was running around the floor in pursuit of the parish cat.

"Does he indeed?" The priest was a very young man with red hair who introduced himself as Father Casey from County Kerry. "Well, we can take care of that now without any trouble." Then, staring hard at his fingernails as if they were offensive to him, he added, "If I might ask, was there a particular reason why you didn't baptize him before?"

That was when Annie May broke down. She cried her eyes out there in the priest's parlor for a solid five minutes before she could say another word. Father Casey was very understanding. He came over and sat beside her and put his arm around her and said, "It's all right, now; it's all right; let it all out." He said this several times. And he gave her his clean white handkerchief to wipe her eyes when she finally showed signs of slowing down. They had a long chat after that, in between retrieving Alphonsus from under chairs and tables and the back of the sofa. Annie May told the whole story of her relationship with Philpot and the circumstances of Alphonsus's arrival and her current miserable situation. Father Casey listened with head down and hands joined, not saying a word. When she finished, he said, "That will do as a confession now. Would you like me to give you absolution?"

"Oh yes, Father, that would be grand." Annie May was enormously relieved to be so quickly quit of her guilty burden.

"Before I can do so," said Father Casey, very gently, "I'll have to ask you to undertake a separation of bed and board from—Philpot, is it? That's an unusual name, now—until after the wedding. It's church law, you see. Well, at least separation of bed; you probably can't afford two flats."

Annie May went home floating on air and waited impatiently for Philpot to come in from work. She had a long wait, for that was the evening Philpot first met Nick. It was just a lucky coincidence, he later told her, bubbling with delight at this new friend he had made and hardly allowing her to get a word in edgeways. He had just stopped in for a quick pint on the way home from work and there was this tall, thin, red-haired fellow standing by the bar. "His name is Nicholas Dunne, and he's from County Carlow. There's something about the man," Philpot said, "that made me instantly recognize a kindred spirit, if you know what I mean."

"I do," said Annie May with resigned disgust. "But right now I want to talk to you about *my* meeting this morning with Father Casey. He'd like very much—"

"He has the kind of intelligence and temperament that suit me very well," Philpot continued. "The two of us spent the evening arguing about politics and religion without ever a cross word being said." He forgot to mention that they had come close to falling out on the politics, Philpot being a strong proponent of the welfare state and Nick turning out to be a diehard conservative. "We're even close on the subject of religion," said he, digging in with great gusto to the dinner that Annie May had kept hot for him. "*He's* a lapsed Catholic too, if you don't mind. 'Mind you, I believe in God,' I told him, so he wouldn't think I'm a complete atheist. 'I believe in Him too,' he said. 'I have no doubt at all about His existence. I just don't like Him.' Now, I thought that was a very astute thing to say."

"It's the bit regarding the lapsed Catholic that I want to talk to you about," said Annie May. And she went on to tell him all about her visit with Father Casey. She emphasized her unhappiness with being in the state of sin, and indeed with Philpot being in a similar condition. And that she was especially distraught because Alphonsus had not been baptized. "So," she said, tapping the table firmly with her finger, "I'm going to obey Father Casey's direction. There will be separate beds from tonight on in this house until you and I are lawfully married and we make a Christian out of himself." She looked Philpot straight in the eye. "So that's it, now." And she got up and walked into the bedroom and shut the door behind her.

If there was one quality about Philpot Emmet that endeared him to some and brought him scorn from others, it was his penchant for avoiding personal conflict. He could and would and did argue till the cows came home about the abstract obligations of politics or religion or whatever the subject matter of discussion. But apply one of those obligations to his own personal life and he would instantly take the line of least resistance, running like a startled rabbit if the way was clear, acquiescing to pressure if flight was not possible. He had run from Creevagh when Annie May found herself in a family way and marriage was required of him. But he could not run now because of his attachment to his son. Alphonsus James Emmet, two years and six months old at this time, was the apple of his father's eye. So Philpot shouted, "Right so" at the bedroom door without waiting to reflect on what he was getting himself into.

"We're to go down to the church for instruction this evening," Annie May told him in the morning, and he on his way out the door. "So be home early."

"Right so," Philpot said again. But in the evening he forgot all about this obligation in the excitement of meeting Miss Joan Fletcher. He had gone into McSweeney's with the sincere intention of having just a quick one to fortify him for the ordeal ahead. And he was putting his empty glass on the bar and saying so long to the lad from Ballindine when in walked Nick with this blonde on his arm. A film star for sure, was Philpot's first reaction. Where in God's name did Nick find her? was his second. As well as the peroxide hair, she had an hourglass figure that her black dress made obvious. And she had that alabaster kind of skin on face and throat that always drove Philpot wild in a woman. "I'd say she's no farmer's daughter from Carlow," he said hurriedly out of the corner of his mouth to the lad from Ballindine. She was from London, Nick informed them. Not that they needed to be told once she opened her mouth. It was an instant disappointment to Philpot, who valued such things, that her accent was closer to Cockney than Oxford. But he forgave her this failing when she smiled at him. That first smile he would never forget. Never in all his days since he became aware of girls as girls had a woman affected him so powerfully so immediately. He was drunk with her presence right from that minute. As the evening wore on he hardly touched his pint, just stood there beside her, listening unheedingly to Nick blathering about the latest misdeeds of the Labour Party, soaking up what he afterwards described to the lad from Ballindine as the indescribable essence of womanhood that she was exuding in his direction. For it was clear from how close she stood to him and the way she looked at him and the glances she threw his way that his lecherous feelings for her were reciprocated.

All that same evening you would never know from Nick's attitude that he took the slightest notice of the fierce attraction that was pulling the pair together. But to Philpot's mortal embarrassment, he brought his attention to the matter when they paid a visit to the jax just before closing time. "I'll thank you, Mr. Emmet, to keep your slimy paws off my bird," was how he put it as he buttoned his fly.

"What do you mean?" Philpot said with that wide-eyed innocence for which he was famous.

"You know very well what I mean, old cock." Nick often affected English ways of speaking. "This one is mine, and I don't want to share her with you or anyone else."

"Well, if that's how you feel," said Philpot, feigning indignation. "What are friends for, anyway?" There was that kind of camaraderie between them already, you see.

At home, Annie May had locked the bedroom door, left no dinner ready, and refused to talk to him. In the morning he left her a note promising on his solemn oath to be home early and ready to go with her to see the priest. And he was. Father Casey was kind but firm. As lapsed Catholics, it was incumbent on them to renew acquaintance with church teaching before receiving the sacraments. "You'll come down here two evenings a week for the next couple of months and I'll give you instruction. At the end of that time you'll go to confession and Communion and then we'll have the wedding and the baptism. In the meantime, no sleeping together." He looked sternly at Philpot as he said this.

On the way home Annie May said, "You'll do it, won't you?"

"I will," he said. "But don't ask me to like it." And for the next couple of months he spent more time than ever at McSweeney's on the nights he didn't have to go to church. That, however, was due more to his infatuation with Joan Fletcher than to compensation for having to listen to Father Casey's homilies. Nick, despite his early admonition, seemed a bit ambivalent about not sharing his bird. He would leave her in Philpot's company, though never in such a way that he couldn't keep an eye on things. Like depositing her in McSweeney's early in the evening, saying he had to step out for a few minutes but he'd be right back, and then not returning for hours. This happened on several occasions, and it drove Philpot to the brink of madness. Joan was so friendly, you see, sitting close to him on the bar stool so that their knees were constantly touching and giving him smiles that would go through him like a dose of salts. What was even worse was that she turned out to be an intelligent woman as well, able to hold her own and more in political discussions and at times leaving him open-mouthed with quotations from historical and literary figures. "She's too good for him," he began to think after a while. But he couldn't make a move because he didn't want a row with Nick. On the fifth occasion that they were left together, however, he could no longer restrain himself. It was an hour since Nick had left, he had lowered a couple of pints, and Joan was joking about the well-known reluctance of Irishmen to marry. In the context it was fairly obvious that she was talking about Nick in particular. "*I'd* marry you in a minute," he said impulsively.

"But you're already married, duckie." She slapped him playfully on the knee.

"I'm not," he denied stoutly, quickly grabbing the pint to overcome his emotion. For he detected in her tone a ray of hope.

"But what about your son? And your wife—whatsername—that you never bring here?"

"Oh, she's not my wife at all," he babbled. "We're not married, you see. That was something that just happened. We all make our mistakes." Now, to give Philpot his fair due, he did feel like the louser he was when he made this terrible statement. It was just that, as he confided later to the lad from Ballindine, he was overcome for the moment by the possibility, however slight it might be, of getting into Joan Fletcher's knickers.

"Now, Philpot," said Joan, "we must be true to those that trust us." But her hand was on his knee as she said it, and the look in her eye was to Philpot's boiling imagination an unequivocal invitation to sin. Unfortunately for him, though quite fortunately for Annie May and young Alphonsus and virtue in general, Nick returned just as his hand began to grope for passage beneath her tight skirt.

"Were you planning a formal wedding or just a quiet one?" Father Casey asked the next evening.

"Oh, a quiet one, Father," Annie May said quickly. "There'll be just ourselves here." Though she had an aunt and an uncle and half a dozen cousins in Middle-sex, she would be too embarrassed to ask them. And she had lied out of shame to the few friends she made in London, letting on that she was married already.

"We can do it all on Saturday morning, then," the priest said. "The christening as well. You'll need two witnesses for the wedding and two sponsors for the bap-tism."

"Who should we get?" Annie May was foolish enough to ask Philpot on the spot.

"Nicholas Dunne and Joan Fletcher," Philpot replied without so much as a pause for reflection.

"Are they good, practicing Catholics?" Father Casey asked.

"Oh, indeed they are, Father. Regular mass-goers." Philpot didn't dare to look at the woman he was about to marry. Annie May said nothing. That she should be reduced to this, who had always wanted a big wedding in Creevagh church and her sister Bridie for bridesmaid. The tears came into her eyes.

"Very good, then. Confession Friday evening at eight o'clock." And Father Casey looked sternly at Philpot.

When the door to the grill slid back, the lad took a deep breath and gripped the armrest tightly. Long expe-rience with confession and confessors in his school life left him in no doubt about what to expect. Especially since repentance was not on his mind, only accommodation. He was doing this for Annie May, but he didn't believe in any of it. And certainly he didn't want to jeopardize his chances with Joan Fletcher by making a good confession. "Bless me, Father, for I have sinned." The nervousness coming out in his voice.

"How long since your last confession?" Father Casey's whisper had the relaxed quality of routine in full swing. Hope burgeoned in Philpot's breast. He might get away lightly after all.

"A bit more than a year, Father." He was not about to admit to the four years and five months he reckoned it to have been since he left Mount St. Joseph's College and the confession box behind him.

"How much more?" But again the whisper was low key.

"Ah, maybe another three, Father." Why did he have to tell that, anyway? He, Philpot Emmet, an avowed agnostic, for God's sake!

"Three months? Three years?"

"Well, most likely years, Father. I'm not sure exactly." He had had a priest for catechism class in Mount St. Joseph's who said that God might strike you dead if you told a lie in the confession box. Like He did to Annanias and Saphira.

"Proceed." Father Casey's voice said *he* might die of boredom any minute now.

"I missed mass a bit, Father. And I didn't get married when I should, and I got drunk a few times. That's about it." Good to get it over with. And he could admit that much anyway, since Annie May would have told the priest already.

"Is that all?" There was a register shift in the priestly whisper.

"That's all I can think of, Father." He remembered the same Cistercian saying you wouldn't be held accountable for what you couldn't remember. "I told lies a few times as well," he threw in for good measure.

"What about the sixth commandment?" Father Casey practically hissed the sibilant.

"The sixth commandment, Father?" Philpot, startled, stalled for time.

"Thou shalt not commit adultery. Have you sinned against the sixth commandment?"

"Oh, no. I never committed adultery, Father. Never." Not one of them had been married as far as he could tell. Except for the girl from Wood Green, and she told him she was married in a registry office, which didn't count.

"Did you commit fornication?"

Philpot clutched the armrest a bit tighter. He was in for it now, and he might as well get it over with. "Ah, yes, Father, a bit." In the end he confessed not only to having had illicit relations with various women for a total well in excess of a hundred times—maybe even a thousand if you included Annie May, which Father Casey said he must—but to taking the Lord's name in vain time out of number, to having missed mass for four consecutive years of Sundays, to having failed to make his Easter duty for the past four years, to having refused to fast and abstain on the days commanded for the past four years, to neglecting to contribute to the support of his pastors for the past four years, to denying his parents the respect he owed them on very many occasions, to being drunk more times than he could remember, to innumerable unchaste thoughts as well as innumerable unchaste deeds with himself, to very many unchaste deeds with others of the female gender that fell short of formal fornication, and to coveting his neighbors' wives many's the time. But he denied with great righteousness ever having stolen anything or even once coveting his neighbors' goods. Father Casey delivered a long, whispered homily and pointedly asked him several times if he were truly sorry for all his sins before pronouncing absolution and letting him go. Philpot staggered from the confessional and collapsed in a pew at the back of the church. Never, he vowed there and then, never in all his days would he ever ever set foot again inside that clerical torture box.

Nick Dunne seemed genuinely pleased and said immediately that he'd be honored to do the honors, as it were. But Joan Fletcher demurred at first about being godmother to Alphonsus. "The priest wouldn't let me, duckie," she said. "Me being an apostate Catholic and all that."

"I told him you are a regular mass-goer." Philpot chortled at this success; he was still smarting from the beating he had taken in the confessional.

"Oh, you are a one!" She slapped him playfully on the behind—they were standing at the bar in McSweeney's— and that was that.

Annie May bought a nice pink frock and flowered hat for the occasion. Philpot wore the blue suit he had bought two months earlier when his old one became too shabby for Joan Fletcher to see him wearing it. They all, including young Alphonsus, sat in the front pew to the left of the altar during nine o'clock mass on Saturday morning. Annie May had Joan keep an eye on the little lad while she went up to Communion. Philpot knelt at the altar rails beside her and closed his eyes and put out his tongue to receive the sacred Host from Father Casey. It meant nothing to him, he told himself; he was doing it just for Annie May. However, on the short walk back to his place a terrible fear took hold of him. It lasted only a few seconds, but in that time he saw himself for what he was with the clear eyes of the Catholic faith that had been instilled in him by his parents and Father Coyne and the Cistercian monks: a heretic desecrating the Body of Christ, an unrepentant sinner crucifying again the Son of God and casting himself feet first into the flaming pit of hell. He knelt in the pew and covered his face with his hands and felt the sweat of his disbelief roll down his forehead. It was just a natural reaction, he told himself. He hadn't been to Communion for years, and the act brought back the emotions of religious fears and doubts he had long since cast off. But he was still in a state of agitation, if not of grace, when the mass ended.

"We'll do the wedding first," Father Casey announced from behind the altar rails after most of the small congregation had left. As he said "I do," Philpot looked up and found Annie May looking at him with eyes of such love that he immediately vowed he would stay away from Joan Fletcher and her kind from now on. They had to sign the register in the sacristy before going down to the baptismal font at the back of the church: Father Casey was a stickler for doing things in the right order and was in no hurry. Unlike Philpot, who had a football match to play at twelve o'clock.

For the christening the priest directed Joan to hold the baby and had Nick stand next to her. He spoke briefly about the importance of baptism and gave a little homily on the duties of godparents: they stood in loco parentis at this moment, he said, and by so doing assumed the lifelong obligation of seeing to the spiritual welfare of this child. The godparents nodded affirmatively at Father Casey and smiled at each other. The godmother hugged the child, and he smiled up at her adoringly. It was noticeable that Alphonsus had taken a liking to the woman. He was well able to stand on his own two feet, of course, but he seemed to enjoy being held by her— Philpot had a fleeting thought that he wouldn't mind being in the lad's place himself—and just watched with big, wide eyes while the priest anointed him and prayed over him and laid hands on him. Philpot looked at his watch: after half ten already and no end in sight to the bloody ceremony. He had fully recovered from his fright at receiving Communion unworthily and was chafing to get going to his football appointment.

It was the tail that caught his attention first. He was standing at right angles to Father Casey and the godparents, and he lowered his head out of bored impatience. His eyes gravitated of their own accord to Joan Fletcher's ankles, as indeed they had done on several occasions already since the interminable rigmarole began. This time he noticed the long, thin, furry yellow object swishing to and fro between the woman's legs just above her black high heels. A cat, was his immediate thought, and he glanced up at Joan's face to see if she was aware of the phenomenon. Then Philpot Emmet screamed. Joan Fletcher was staring down at his son with a look of such intense evil as to merit the term *diabolical*. And from her blonde hair protruded a pair of long, curved yellow horns.

They tell you that people are often paralyzed by fear and can't move a muscle in the direst emergencies. Well, not Philpot Emmet. The hairs on his nape were extended, his toes were curled, and his skin was blanched. But having screamed one long, terrified scream and glanced quickly at Nick for help and found that he too was wearing horns and the devil's own visage, Philpot the footballer took over. He lunged at Joan Fletcher, knocking Nick Dunne aside with his shoulder, and snatched Alphonsus from Satan's arms like a football from the hands of an opponent. In his charge he caught Father Casey with his hip and sent the man of God reeling and his holy water splashing. The last thing he remembered as he raced out the door was Annie May's scream.

The

Black

Gander

CATHERINE Ryan was sick of England. She was tired of London's crowded Underground and dirty streets and the packed rowhouses of Finsbury Park. She hated working behind the perfume counter at Schweitzer's, even though her friend Molly kept telling her how lucky she was to have such a nice, clean job when she, Molly, had to slave eight hours a day in a filthy canning factory. Anyway, another thing Catherine hated was having to share this miserable little flat with Molly, who, though a good sort in many ways, was terribly untidy and snored and had a habit of borrowing her things without permission. So when the letter came from Thomas on St. Patrick's Day pleading with her to come home, she was tempted.

How he ever found her address she didn't know, but there it was in his ever-so-neat handwriting on a light blue envelope. The writing paper was blue as well. "I'm getting old," he wrote. "I need a woman to take care of me. If you'll come back we'll let bygones be bygones. I'll sign the place over to you. I can't run it on my own anymore. Your old black gander is still alive; I've been taking care of him for you. Heneghan is gone, for good this time; we had a falling out last year. . . ."

But it was well she knew what a slippery character was the same Thomas. "Send me a copy of the will," she wrote back to him.

"It'll be waiting for you when you get here," he replied immediately. Catherine resigned herself to living out her life behind Schweitzer's perfume counter. Until she got one of those rare letters from Maura Higgins at the beginning of June.

"I thought you should know that Thomas is dying," Maura wrote. "The doctor said he has only a month to live." Within the week Catherine was on the boat home. He was in Castlebar hospital dying of lung cancer, caused most likely, said the doctor, by his lifelong habit of smoking Players Navy Cut cigarettes. They sent him home with her to die; there was nothing more they could do for him, and they needed the hospital bed. On the way up in the ambulance she asked him about the will.

"'Tis all taken care of," was all he could get breath to rasp. In three days he was dead. The funeral was on a Saturday. When she got back from the graveyard she wrote to the solicitors inquiring about the will. That same day Phelim O'Brien arrived home more than a month early for his summer holidays.

He came almost unannounced. A telegram was delivered to the house by Michael Joe Lynch, the postmaster's youngest son, at half one in the afternoon to say Phelim would be on the six o'clock train from Dublin that evening and would someone please meet him at the station. The heart turned crossways on his poor mother.

"I knew it," she wailed. "I knew it. The sciatica has been killing me this past week, and that's a sure sign of bad news." It wasn't of course that she minded having him home; it was that she knew they never got holidays this early, so his coming must mean he was in trouble. With only a year to go before the great day, she was terribly afraid something would happen to stop it. The ordination of her son was the dream of her life, the focus of her prayers, and the guarantee of her salvation: Could the Almighty turn the mother of a priest away from the gates of Heaven? But she had an awful fear it would never come to pass. She didn't have any particular reason that she could put a finger on, or that would make sense if she tried to put words to it. Nevertheless, a mother had a sixth sense about these things: everyone said what a great boy her Phelim was and what a fine priest he would make; only Nellie O'Brien knew the fearful son she had raised and the terrible coward he could be when the occasion allowed. She had nightmares of him stalling at the final fence like a racehorse at Beecher's Brook.

She was partly right, mind you. Phelim did indeed have the jitters coming up to ordination. More precisely, the lowering approach of the subdiaconate was inducing incessant cramps in his stomach. Although this, the first of the major orders, didn't confer much power—unlike the last of the minor orders that made him an exorcist—it did place on the recipient a fearsome burden. There was a moment in the ceremony when the bishop called on the ordinandi gathered around him in the episcopal sanctuary to take a symbolic step forward and by so doing assume the lifelong and irrevocable obligation of celibacy. To be sure, as a member of the religious Congregation of the Holy Ghost and the Immaculate Heart of Mary, Phelim had already taken a vow of perpetual chastity. But that wasn't the same thing, you see. You could, if the situation required it, be released by the Pope from a vow of perpetual chastity. Which happened occasionally to scholastics who left after taking final vows but before receiving major orders. However, there was no power on earth that would release a man from the celibacy obligation he undertook at the subdiaconate. And despite nine years of religious life and monastic discipline and fierce dedication to the Holy Virtue, Phelim O'Brien's libido, though he would never admit it even to himself, was as lively as it had been the day he entered the novitiate. And to make matters worse he had been plagued for the past year by memories of Catherine McGrath—or Catherine Ryan, as she was since she had married that old codger Thomas Ryan. Ever since he heard she had run away to England, he couldn't get her out of his mind. And not sweet, romantic thoughts, either. Images of the most impure kind, of glistening flesh and private parts and obscene acts. He didn't know where they were coming from; they had to be straight from Satan himself, a last-ditch effort to destroy his vocation. He countered them with prayer and mortification and cold showers, though he didn't seek counsel from his spiritual director lest his temptations be thought weakness and a sign of unfitness for ordination.

Very likely it was this failure to acknowledge his libidinous status quo, coupled with his fierce determination to be ordained a priest and his equally fierce terror of taking on irreversible spiritual eunuchhood, that gave him the ulcers. Not bad enough to be operated on but serious enough for the doctor to prescribe total rest for a couple of months and for his director to send him home early for the summer holidays with orders to observe absolute peace and quiet.

He told his mother about the ulcers but not, of course, about their cause. She was relieved at first but then worried out loud if he were going to be well enough for ordination. A priest had to be in good health if he was to be any use on the missions. Then, slyly, she suggested that maybe because of his health they'd put him teaching in one of the colleges here at home instead. Most of the Holy Ghost Fathers went to Africa, and Mrs. O'Brien didn't like the idea of her son spending the rest of his life on the Dark Continent.

Catherine Ryan went to first mass on Sunday. She was staying home for good, and though she wasn't much of a Catholic anymore, it was better to be seen going to mass than to be talked about for not going. In England she sometimes went and sometimes didn't. The first year when she went to confession to do her Easter duty, the priest had refused her absolution because she wouldn't promise there and then to go back to her lawful husband. So she hadn't been to confession since. But her heritage was still within her, and there was a certain comfort in kneeling near the back on the women's side and breathing the stale air of Creevagh church. The sight of her Phelim striding up the aisle to the front of the men's side was so unexpected that it brought out the goose pimples in her. It also made her want to cry. Which she did, very quietly, her face buried in her hands, hoping no one would notice. Nine years since they cycled to school in Kilmolara together. A marriage with no love in it to old Thomas Ryan. A fling into adultery with Reddy Ryan that might have brought about that lad's tragic death, the Lord have mercy on him. A couple of wretched relationships with a Scottish rugby player and a Welsh train driver during her three years in England. But could any single one of these, or the sum total of them all for that matter, banish, or even diminish, her love for Phelim O'Brien? Wasn't that the truth, now! Wasn't he the only lad she had ever really wanted? The only one that could calm the restless twitching of her body and her mind, God help her. Why did they have to stay single, anyway? Strapping young fellows, heirs to the flesh, as the gospel said, as much as anyone else. But forbidden, forever if you don't mind, to do what nature was forever screaming out for. And indeed, she had felt that passion in him the day he came up to see her before she married Thomas. Well she remembered it. When he challenged her to tickle him and let her feel his manhood and kiss his lips. Wasn't it she, not he, that had backed off before they got in too deep to get out? Arrah, why did she stop that day, anyway? She had had him by the bollocks, for Christ's sake. But she did let him go, the more fool she. Well, she wouldn't do it again. Just give her one more chance, O Lord. Blasphemy to pray like that, wasn't it? But she didn't care. She wanted her Phelim all to herself, and she could never have him. Yesterday at feeding time the old black gander, her Phelim gander, as she called him, wasn't eating, just lying on the ground like he was ready to die. That was an omen if ever there was one.

She felt the tears again at the consecration of the mass, when Father Coyne briefly raised the Body of Christ high over his head for all to see, to the triumphant clanging of the mass-server's bell. He'd soon be ordained, and the only flesh he would thenceforth hold would be that of his Lord. Why couldn't he raise up the body of Catherine Ryan? Become one flesh with her instead of the Christ? She was wicked to think those thoughts. But didn't *He* have enough brides? Or grooms, or whatever they were to Him? He could have all the rest; just let Catherine Ryan have her Phelim O'Brien. At Communion time she envied the people who went up to receive, not being able to go herself in her state of sin. God forgive her, she would be more thrilled at the touch of *his* fingers placing the Host on her tongue than she would be about receiving the flesh of her Savior.

Outside afterwards, she waited at the bottom of the steps near the gate. A few older men raised their caps ever so slightly as they passed without so much as looking at her. Grudging respect for Thomas Ryan's widow, she well knew, not acknowledgment of herself. Several women went by, ignoring her completely. There would be a lot more of that in the months to come; they would never forgive her for walking out on Thomas.

Phelim dropped into the sacristy after mass to pay his

respects to his parish priest. Father Coyne was heading down to Nephin after breakfast to visit his mother, who would be ninety years of age next week, God spare her health, so he only had time for a few words. Phelim explained the reason for his being home so early, and the priest, without so much as pausing in the act of removing his vestments, said, "Perseverance. Perseverance is what it's all about." He shook hands again and went back out into the sanctuary to say his thanksgiving, without inviting his protégé down to the house for breakfast as he sometimes had in the past.

Phelim was folding the ends of his trousers inside his socks for the cycle home when he heard the woman call out a quiet, "Hello, Mr. O'Brien." It was, he thought, a sad reflection on his inability to control his thoughts that the voice sounded like Catherine Ryan's. He turned quickly, as much to dispel the hallucination as to see who it really was, and found himself staring at Catherine Ryan.

"Good God! Where did *you* come from?" So utterly different a greeting from what his fantasy meetings with her usually evoked. He had thought she was in England.

"I'm home again. This time to stay." Standing on the far side of her bicycle, dressed in a somber gray suit and tiny black hat pertly perched on the left side of her head. And with a challenging look in those green eyes that dared him to something.

"That's good." He paused. "I suppose." He had the sensation of walking on a buttered floor and being about to upend any second. "How's Thomas?"

"I buried him yesterday." As dispassionately as if recounting the sale of a bullock.

"Well, is that a fact? I'm sorry to hear it." Though he didn't expect there would be much grief on her part. No one at home had mentioned the man's death, of course, which was in keeping with his family's general policy of silence regarding Catherine.

"I didn't expect to see you so soon." She wheeled the bike a little closer. "You usually come in August, don't you?"

"You have a good memory." He hadn't seen her now for three years, since just after Reddy's death. "They said I needed a bit of rest, so they packed me off home early." Despite the gray clothes she looked more ravishing than ever. Something to do with the angle of the hat, maybe, and the way her hair was done, and the makeup; she was more slender, too, than he remembered her.

"You do look a bit pale. Worry, I suppose; you were always a great worrier." Her smile and the way she looked at him suggested shared secrets. "You're thinner too. Are they feeding you decently?"

"It's the asceticism. All that fasting and praying. You know how it is with us monks!" The cynicism of the theologian: a couple of years ago he would never have dreamed of making light of the monastic way of life.

"You haven't got tired of it all yet?" There was a weary kind of resignation in the question.

"It's my chosen path," he countered. "Tiredness has nothing to do with it."

"Well, you're much to be admired." Then, looking around, she added, "I suppose I'd better be going. We wouldn't want people talking about us, would we?" But just as she placed a foot on the pedal, she turned. "Would you come back to visit me one of these days?"

He was hoping she'd ask. He was afraid she'd ask. But he didn't know how to respond. More correctly, he knew how he should respond and how he wanted to respond but couldn't reconcile the two. "Maybe," he said, the commitment of cowards.

"Ah, do!" Genuine pleading. "Come Wednesday afternoon and I'll make a rhubarb tart." And she rode off. He walked back into the church and waited and prayed for five minutes so he wouldn't catch up with her on the way home.

Three long days passed till Wednesday afternoon, but then he didn't come anyway. And the black gander lay in a corner of the barn, not able to die and not able to rise. Catherine was tempted to put him out of his misery but couldn't get up the courage to do the deed. Thursday, going on three, just when she was about to go into town, Phelim arrived on his bicycle. "I had given up on you," she told him. "I thought for sure you weren't coming."

"I almost didn't." His eyes were washed out, she thought; the look of a man deep in worry.

"Were you afraid?" A touch of anger coming out at him for leaving her dangling in despair.

"You could say that, I suppose." He didn't even smile but plopped into a chair near the fire, though it was a warm day.

"Afraid of what? That I'd bite you?" She wasn't going to make it easy for him.

"Maybe. I have an ulcer, you know, and I'm not supposed to do any worrying, and I worried myself sick over whether I should come over to see you. And then I worried about how to get here without Mammy knowing it: you know how she feels about you. So all in all I haven't been doing the stomach any favors."

She sat by the table, at a safe distance from him. "Well, there's nothing to be afraid of here, I can tell you. I'm not going to bite you today." She arched an eyebrow at him. "Amn't I a respectable widow woman now, anyway? And isn't visiting widows and orphans one of the corporal works of mercy? So there you are!" But her smile was impudent.

"It isn't you I'm afraid of," he said, unsmiling, "but me."

She nodded vigorously. "The trouble with you, Phelim, is that you never let yourself go. You're like a steaming kettle except you have nowhere to let the steam get out. If you're not careful, one of these days you'll explode." He was watching her, listening intently, but made no attempt to respond. "And speaking of steaming kettles, would you like a cup of tea?" She got up, went over to the range, picked up the black iron kettle from the floor, and put it on the burner. "I've had water in it all morning in case you came."

"If you wouldn't mind, Catherine, I'd prefer a cup of milk." He grimaced. "The ulcer, you know. They tell me the milk is the best thing for it."

He looked beautiful sitting there in his clerical garb. And she was ridiculously thrilled at the sound of her name coming from his lips. "Ah, yes, of course. Milk! Creamy and soft and white and smooth: the perfect food for flesh and blood. I read that somewhere; I think it was an advertisement." Plucking the kettle roughly from the range and putting it back on the floor. "I'll get you some from the pantry." She took a cup from the dresser and went out the kitchen door and across the hall to the tiny, cool, dark room where she kept the milk and butter. She filled the cup from the jug that was fresh from the morning milking and brought it to him. "And maybe a bit of rhubarb tart?" She smiled at him.

"I could be persuaded." And this time he smiled back, that half-shy, half-impudent grin that had always set her toes tingling.

She retrieved the tart from the lower dresser shelf and put a generous wedge on a plate, which she placed on the table. "Come on over here now and eat it." She sat next to him and watched. Just being this close teased her to touch him, his arm, his face, any part of his body. When he was finished, she said, "I have a gander that's sick out in the barn. I thought maybe if you could bless him he might get well." Trying hard to keep a straight face.

"Well now," he said, very solemnly, "I don't have any particular power to bless things yet. That only comes with ordination. Of course, if he was possessed by the devil I could do something about that, since I *have* been ordained an exorcist."

"Maybe you can do that, then." She got up immediately and headed out the back door. But when they looked inside the barn there was no gander to be seen. They searched everywhere, behind machinery and carts and horse's harness, and then tramped through the hay shed, and after that they looked around the entire yard, but the dying bird had vanished. "I don't know where he could have gone," Catherine said, bewildered. "He wasn't even able to walk for the past two days."

"Maybe the fox got him," Phelim suggested.

"The fox only comes at night. He's like the devil that way," she added maliciously.

"Does the devil only come out at night?" He was still peering around the yard, but then he turned and stared straight at her.

"That's what my granny used to tell us." She stopped her searching and gave him her full attention. Just his gazing at her was having a terrible effect on her entire body. "The devil is like the fox, she'd say," she babbled. "He comes at night to steal the souls of children who don't say their prayers going to bed. Do you think that's true?" But she couldn't look straight at him for fear she'd laugh.

"I don't know," he said. "Do you say your prayers going to bed?"

"I used to, but I'm afraid not too much anymore. Do you believe in the devil?"

"Well, I do think he's a force to be reckoned with in this world." He said this in a very priestly way. "How about you?"

"I don't know what I believe in anymore." She stared back the fields as if she might spot the old gander grazing there. "I sometimes wake up in the middle of the night in a sweat because I'm in the state of mortal sin and I'm afraid I'm going to die right there and then and go straight to hell. And I promise God if He spares me I'll go to confession on Saturday. But when Saturday comes I can't bring myself to go." She looked at him. "Would *you* hear my confession, Phelim?" That thought gave her a terrible immediate jolt of impure pleasure.

"Sure," he said, and the shy, impudent grin was back. "Kneel down there in the cow dung in your nice pink frock and we'll get it over with."

"I'm not codding, Phelim." She raised her dress as if about to get down on her knees there and then. Instantly his face turned serious.

"Don't," he said urgently. "You know I can't."

"Why not?" The thought of telling her Phelim about all the terrible sins she committed with poor Reddy, the Lord have mercy on him, was exciting her. "You're almost a priest now, aren't you?" Oh God! Her thoughts right this minute were serious matter for confession in themselves.

"Almost doesn't count. You have to be ordained to have that power. And I'm not there yet." You could feel the pain in his tone.

"Well, anyway!" She gave him her best smile. "You wouldn't want to hear *my* confession. You'd die of embarrassment, I'd say."

"You can't embarrass a priest." He said it stiffly, as if the very idea offended him. "By the end of our theology studies we'll have heard it all."

"But that's all books. I'm talking about life." She felt a sudden impatience with his starchy attitude. "I'll tell you something, Phelim: you'll go to your grave without ever really knowing what's under my frock, if you know what I mean." And she turned and headed back towards the house.

"The physician doesn't have to suffer the disease to know the cure." He caught up to her.

"So we're all diseases to you, are we?" She didn't slow down. "Is that what we are, Phelim O'Brien?" She was getting hysterical; she could feel it coming on.

"That was just a metaphor. I—"

"Feck the metaphors! Why can't you talk plain English for once in your life?"

"Some things can't be explained in plain English."

"Faith, you have a point there." She stopped suddenly just outside the back door. "And I'm going to show you a thing that can't be explained in plain English." She caught his arm and half dragged him back inside the kitchen, down the hall, and into her bedroom. "Sit down here." She pushed him onto the bed. He sat obediently, mouth half open, squinting up at her in a look that combined puzzlement with a little fear. When she kicked off her good shoes and stood before him in her bare feet his head jerked back, though he didn't move. But when she lifted the hem of her frock and started undoing the buttons he made to get up. She leaned over and pushed him back down. "Patience! It takes a while to loosen all these buttons." She folded the frock carefully and laid it on the chair by the bedside before looking at him again. His head was away back now, and he was staring at the ceiling. "Look at me," she said. And he did, like a child obeying his mother. She pulled her petticoat over her head. He was still looking. "This is a brassiere." She placed her hands over her covered breasts. "And these are knickers." She looked down at the tight white garment covering her middle. "Have you ever seen a woman in this state before, in your entire life?"

"No!" He looked down at the floor.

"Look at me," she said again. And again he did. And though his face turned red, he didn't stop looking when she put her hands behind her back and snapped loose the brassiere and slipped it off and dropped it on top of her frock and petticoat. "Have you ever seen these before?"

"Oh, God!" It sounded like the steam from a train at Paddington station.

"Have you?" She demanded.

"Never!" This time looking straight at her eyes. There was a distinct quiver in his voice. "Don't, please," he pleaded when she began to slip off the knickers. But he didn't move, and when she straightened with them in her hand and dropped them onto the rest of her clothes he was still looking at her with eyes half closed and mouth half open, as if he were in mortal agony. But he didn't so much as flinch when she stepped forward and leaned over, her breasts hanging right before his face. Or resist when she took his hands and raised them till they were pushing those breasts against the wall of her chest. Not even when she traced his fingers against her inner thighs and brushed them firmly against the dark red hair between did he so much as make a gesture of pulling away.

"Now tell me, Phelim O'Brien," hauling him to his feet and holding him close, her breath coming short with passion, "what's wrong with this body that you don't want to see it or touch it?"

"Oh, God help me, I do want you!" Cri de coeur from a tortured soul. And he wrapped himself around her and held her so tightly for so long that she thought she might asphyxiate. She pushed him back gently on the bed then and undressed him and caressed him and got him inside her just in time. Afterwards they lay quietly, saying nothing, just touching and clutching, stroking and feeling. Until Phelim began to cry. It began as a single soft sniffle so that she thought he merely needed to blow his nose. But the sniffles multiplied in strength and number and mutated to sobs till his entire body shuddered and bubbled like a pig's pot on the boil. When she tried gently to console him with arms and hands and lips he pushed her roughly away. Eventually he sat up and got his legs to the floor, his back to her as she lay watching. "Sorry," she said softly.

He dressed without answering and walked around the bed in silence. Then in the doorway he turned and, staring at the floor, said in a voice croaking with phlegm and disgust, "Goodbye."

Again she said, "Sorry! So sorry. I didn't mean to hurt you." But when he was gone and she went back the fields to feed the geese, and the old black gander was the first to come waddling towards her, neck outstretched and beak wide open, she grabbed a large potato from her bucket and flung it viciously at him.

God's

Anointed

THE celebration was being planned for a month, but
the go-ahead was not official till Father Coyne announced it from the pulpit. "One of the greatest
joys a parish can experience is the homecoming of one of
its own as a newly anointed priest of God," said the
parish priest of Creevagh at last mass on the second Sunday in July. "It gives me great pleasure to tell you that I
received a telegram just before I came on the altar saying
that Phelim O'Brien was ordained by the archbishop of
Dublin this morning. Father Phelim will be home with us
at seven o'clock this evening, and I invite you to join me
in meeting him here in front of the church. Tomorrow
morning at nine o'clock he will celebrate his first holy

mass at this altar. I strongly urge all who can to attend: there is a special grace in the first mass and blessing of a newly ordained priest. Also, a reception will be given by the Ladies' Welcoming Committee in Father Phelim's honor at the parish hall tomorrow evening at eight o'-clock, to which all are invited. Tea and refreshments will be served."

"You'd think he was the crown prince of Creevagh," said Martin Mangan a few nights later back at Gannon's. There were a few who snorted into their pints at this statement, suspecting the same Martin Mangan of harboring sympathies toward royalty. But in any case it was a fair description of the new priest's status. A banner strung across the road outside the parish hall said, "Welcome Home Father Phelim," and when he arrived on Sunday evening it was in a motorcade of family and friends who had gone up to Dublin to witness the sacred event. Father Coyne was at the head of the welcoming party in front of the church, in surplice and soutane, attended by his mass-servers in their surplices and soutanes and surrounded by a fairly decent crowd of parishioners. The Creevagh football players were there in togs, complete with ball and flag, to greet their former teammate. Mrs. Addis stood in front of the girls' choir, and they burst into a sacred song of welcome the minute Father Phelim stepped out of his motorcar. When they finished, a general blessing from the new priest brought all to their knees. After which the cheering could be heard halfway to Kilmolara, led by the footballers' *hip, hip, hooray!* Father Coyne made a short speech of welcome, and then all adjourned into the church for Benediction of the Blessed Sacrament, given by the newly anointed one.

In all of this the proud parents had pride of place. Even Father Coyne stood back to let them be first into the church. It was their day almost as much as their son's. As was the next morning, when they and their other children occupied the front benches for the first mass. Creevagh church was more than half full when their newly ordained offspring processed onto the altar in his glittering white vestments, preceded by six red-and-white-clad mass-servers. "Faith, it isn't long since he was a mass-server himself," Maggie Ruane, halfway back, whispered loudly to Brigid Moloney. The young priest pronounced the Latin cadences of the sacred ritual with a sharp, clear diction and a good deal more slowly than Father Coyne's rapid patter. After he read the gospel and reverently kissed the missal, he turned to face the congregation. A quick general cough preceded the great silence of expectancy.

"My dear fellow parishioners of Creevagh," said Father Phelim O'Brien, "I want to thank you all most sincerely for being here this morning to celebrate this holy mass with me." Then his pause was longer than needed for his words to sink in: although he had prepared his talk with the greatest care several weeks ago and had memorized it and practiced it, yet now he felt in danger of forgetting the rest. "I owe the greatest debt of all to my parents," he managed to remember, "without whose word and example and encouragement and support I would not be here today. I'd like to thank, too, my brothers and sisters for all their help to me over the years." He was getting into his stride now; the worst was over. "My most sincere gratitude of course goes to Father Coyne, my spiritual mentor and counselor, whose unfailing guidance and direction have kept me from straying from the straight and narrow path of holiness." Three down and one to go. "And let me not forget the enormous debt I owe to my former teacher, Mr. Addis Emmet, for fostering my vocation with his stress on duty and discipline and fidelity to the faith of our fathers. Not to mention encouraging me to play football at an early age." An unrehearsed quip, this last, that brought the first stirring of life from the congregation. Oh, God, he forgot to thank everyone else! "And finally I'd like to thank you all, every parishioner of this parish, from the bottom of my heart. Never once have I received anything but kindness and good example from any of you; never once has anyone said or done anything to hinder me from following the path that God has laid out for me." So what about Catherine Ryan? God forgive him, he couldn't very well retract what had slipped from his mouth. But he'd better stop now before he took any more liberties with the truth. "In the name of the Father and of the Son and of the Holy Ghost. Amen." And he turned quickly to face the altar.

A whole year of mass practice gave him a feeling of comfort with the sacred liturgy. Until he reached the consecration, where it was not merely a matter of familiarity with ritual but of mental focus and intention of will and exact adherence to syllables and words. It would be so easy to lose concentration or pronounce the sacred text improperly or forget a phrase and thereby render the holy mass not only sinful but invalid. As many as 140 mortal sins could be committed by the minister of the Eucharist, said the moral theologians and canonists, so it behooved the celebrant to observe the utmost care and scrupulosity. Phelim paused to recollect and assure himself that he was fully conscious of what he was doing be-- fore he uttered the dread words, *Hoc est enim Corpus Meum.* And yet, as he raised the Host for adoration by the congregation, it required the most profound act of his will to believe that what had previously been simple un- leavened bread in his hand was now by his mere words transformed into the Body of Christ. So shaken was he by this miracle and that of his consecration of wine into the Sacred Blood that his mind could scarcely attend to the remainder of the Canon. And indeed the rest of the mass was ever after but a blur in his memory. He could recall quite clearly placing the sacred Host on the tongue of his mother, but all else, until he found himself back in the sacristy, was a fog he could never dispel. Indeed, if he had not been reminded by Father Coyne, he would have removed his vestments immediately instead of returning to the sanctuary for the ceremony of the First Blessing.

The entire congregation flocked to the altar rails. The First Blessing had a special power, you see, coming fresh from pious young hands that were as yet unsullied by worldly contamination. If it wouldn't be irreverent, one might say it was like the kiss of a virgin. Father Phelim stood before each parishioner in turn, his long fingers joined tightly while he intoned the benediction in Latin. When he said *In nomine Patris,* the big right hand cut a sign of the cross out of the air. And each time he finished the prayer, those newly anointed palms pressed down on the recipient as bearers of God's special blessing. He touched old gray hair and young dark hair and bright red hair like his own, and the shoulders of women and the pates of bald men. He raised hands over those he had revered as figures of authority: Addis Emmet and Mrs., and Paddy Gannon, and Jack Higgins; people as old as his parents, such as Bernie the postman and Clare Mulligan and Jimmy McTigue; as well as lads and girls his own age. A particular surprise was Seamus Laffey, whom he thought was in England. "We just got married last week," Seamus whispered, grinning and nodding at Eileen Maille kneeling beside him.

"I'll talk to you after," Phelim whispered back. But he quickly forgot his old friend, for even as he blessed his mind was enveloping itself in a daze of doubt over the validity of the consecration he had just performed. What if he didn't have the requisite intention when he said the words? Did the congregation receive the Body of Christ or mere bread from his hands? The clouds of worry swirled and grew and hovered over him for the rest of the morning, all through the congratulations of neighbors and friends outside the church, through the triumphant return home to Knockard and the lavish celebratory breakfast in the O'Brien parlor. Not until he was allowed to retire to his room in midafternoon to rest and recite his breviary did he have a chance to review his sacred actions and his current state of soul. *How can you ever be sure?* kept ringing in his brain. *The reasonable action of a reasonable man,* sang the counterpoint of his moral professor. But were his actions reasonable this morning? Was he so distracted by the grandness of the occasion that his intention was lacking? Was he so full of pride in his newly exalted state that he could not focus on the awful act he had to perform? Eventually, exhausted, he removed jacket and collar and lay on the bed and slept.

Inside the parish hall, the Ladies' Welcoming Committee raced in all directions like ants on an anthill, laying out the minerals and plates of home-baked breads and cakes and scones and tarts. They had spent the day cleaning the hall and decorating it with streamers and bunting and banners and putting the tables in place and covering them with borrowed tablecloths. By half seven, well before the O'Brien clan arrived, the hall was on the way to being full: the mere mention of refreshments guaranteed a social success for the evening. Even some of the Gannon's crowd turned up, despite the reception's lack of intoxicating lubricants. "Sure, abstinence only makes the heart grow fonder, they say," Pat Moloney said, raising his cup of tea in informal toast to the young priest.

"I'd say his football days are over," Thomas Ruane observed sagely.

"Do you think?" said Pat. "There was a lad on the Ballindine team changed his name after he was ordained and kept on playing unbeknownst to the archbishop. So there you are, now!" He winked at Thomas.

"He's going off to Africa anyway. They don't play football in the jungle, I heard them say." Thomas sipped his tea with a grimace. "He'll be out there in his white soutane and he surrounded by naked black childer, like them pictures you see in the *Missionary Annals*."

"Faith, you wouldn't catch me among all those black lads," said Francie Madden, who along with Paddy Moran had just joined their table. "They'd be as likely as not to have you for supper some evening, as the fellow said." Francie bit into a scone.

"Did you hear the one about the Franciscan they put

in the pot?" Paddy Moran asked solemnly. "The chief came along and said, 'You can't boil him, he's a friar.'" Francie and Paddy guffawed, but the two older men stared at them without comprehension.

"They say the women go 'round naked as the day they were born," Francie said, staring at his mineral bottle.

"So that's why he's going out there!" Paddy Moran thumped the table with his fist, causing Thomas Ruane's tea to spill. "Our Phelim always did have an eye for the girls, mind you." He and Francie sniggered with their heads down.

"There's no call at all now for that kind of smutty talk." Pat Moloney stared sternly at the young libertines. "If them two fellows over there heard ye, you'd be for it, let me tell you."

The two fellows in question were Father Coyne and Addis Emmet. They sat with Mrs. Addis at a table in front of the stage, heads close together, talking quietly, though Pat Moloney would have been surprised at some of the language they used. "Bleddy fellow!" Addis was saying with fierce intensity at the very moment he was being pointed out.

"And you're sure now, Addis, that they're gone?" Though the parish priest's scowl left little doubt as to what he himself believed.

"Annie May came back to the house yesterday evening and the creature—" Addis stopped suddenly.

"Are you ready for some more tea, Father?" A Welcoming Committee lady standing before them brandishing a smile and a teapot.

"Maybe just a sup, Kitty, thank you very much."

"Anyway," said Addis, after Kitty filled their cups,

"Annie May was in a terrible state, the poor girl. 'He's gone,' was the first thing she said walking in the door. 'Again?' I said, thinking it was young Fonsy who had wandered; he's forever going off across the fields and forgetting to come back. 'Philpot,' she said, and she started crying. It took us a while to get it out of her, but it seems that when she got home from last mass—they have to go to separate masses now since the new baby arrived— Philpot wasn't there."

"I knew straight away yesterday morning something was wrong," said Mrs. "Philpot didn't go to Holy Communion. It was the first Sunday he missed ever since he came home." She bowed her head and pressed her fingertips tightly together. "I should have asked him what was the matter. He might still be here if I did." The strangled sound from somewhere inside her could have been a sob.

"Anyway," Addis continued as if he had not been interrupted, "Annie May found a note on the kitchen table saying Philpot had left the baby with Mrs. Maille. But not another word, mind you, to say where the wretched fellow was going."

"Well, well! Isn't he the terrible blackguard!" And Father Coyne clucked a mixture of outrage and sympathy.

"When I get my hands on him . . ." The fierce eye of Addis Emmet left no doubt as to the fate of his erring offspring. "So Annie May went down to Maille's to get the baby. But they didn't know where Philpot was going either. Then she walked over to Coleman's: young Tommie has an old motorbike and Philpot helps him work on the engine. And that's when she found out: Tommie said Philpot had come by in the Morris Minor and taken his sister Teresa for a spin. And neither of the pair has been seen since."

"Ah, good God Almighty!" Deep pastoral anguish in the priest's tone. "And sure the Coleman girl is only a slip of a thing. Hardly out of the convent school."

"I really should have asked him," Mrs. lamented again.

"He'll be the sorriest . . ." Addis was off again.

"Could I have a word with you, Father?" Timmy Mulligan bent low, whispering in the parish priest's ear.

"Certainly, Timmy." Father Coyne turned and looked benevolently at his wealthiest parishioner.

"Could we talk in private, Father?" Without so much as a glance at Addis or Mrs. Then, standing over in the corner to the right of the stage, a little bit away from listening ears, Timmy said urgently, "Sorry to disturb you, Father, but I wanted to tell you the good news myself before you heard it from anyone else: I'm going to get married."

Father Coyne had a soft spot for this man ever since the matter of Paddy Gannon's grandchild: in making amends for Martin Mulligan's sin, Timmy had shown himself to be a man of integrity. "That's wonderful, now, Timmy; I'm delighted to hear it. The very best of luck to you." And parish priest and parish tycoon cordially shook hands.

"She wants the wedding as soon as possible," murmured Timmy. And then, in a rush, as if the details were distasteful to him, he went on, "But I told her it'd take a bit of time: we'll first have to get all kinds of certificates and permissions and fill out forms and statements and the like. Isn't it true for me, Father?"

"Slow down now, for a minute!" Father Coyne did, for him, an unusual thing: he put his hands in his trousers pockets. "A lot depends on where the bride is currently domiciled." He straightened his shoulders and looked Mulligan in the eye. "And since you haven't yet told me who the lucky woman is, I don't have a good answer to your question."

"Sorry, Father. I've been going around all evening like a clocking hen, from the minute I got back from Dublin. I went up there this morning and proposed to her and she said yes and the brain has been like a scrambled egg ever since." He pulled at his tie as if it were choking him.

"Understandably," Father Coyne said in a most kindly way. "Quite understandably in the circumstances, I suppose. And who was it now that you proposed to, if I might ask?"

Timmy stared at him. "Catherine, of course. Who else?"

"Catherine!" The priest's right hand came out of his pocket and massaged his chin. "I know at least three Catherines in this parish, but I don't think any one of them is eligible. So it must be someone from outside. Do I know her, by any chance?"

"Catherine Ryan, Father. I thought everybody knew about us. . . ." Timmy's expression bespoke deep disappointment that gossip so important had failed to reach such august ears.

"You don't say! Well! Well! Well! Catherine Ryan! And when did all this come about?"

"Ah, sure, it started last year when she came to me for advice on selling her place. She said women can't handle those kinds of things. And we've been going strong ever since."

"I see, faith. She said that? Isn't that interesting! Well, it'll be a great wedding for Creevagh, for sure. And God knows we could do with one."

Timmy cleared his throat and folded his arms and rocked back and forth on his heels. "Catherine wants to get married in Dublin," he blurted.

Father Coyne's eyebrows lowered immediately to the danger level. "Not at all, man! Why would she want to go and do a thing like that?" He stared challengingly at Timmy. "Sure every man, woman, and child in the parish of Creevagh has been waiting for years to see Timmy Mulligan get married. You can't disappoint them now, can you?"

Timmy stared at the floor. "It's Catherine, Father. If it was up to me . . . But you know how the women are when they get an idea into their heads!"

The priest stood in silence for a minute. Then he waved a hand at the noisy crowd around them. "There'll be a lot of people who won't be happy about this. Where is Catherine living now?"

"She has a flat in Terenure, Father."

The priest shrugged his shoulders. "If she's domiciled in Dublin, I suppose there isn't much we can do about it. You'll want me to do the honors, I suppose?" Father Coyne's tone left no doubt as to who would perform the ceremony. "Of course we'll need the permission of the parish priest of her parish."

Timmy's head, which had raised with the good news of the priest's acquiescence to a Dublin wedding, promptly dropped again. "Well, it's like this, Father: she wants Phelim—Father Phelim—to do it. But of course I wouldn't ask him without getting your permission first." This with all the authority of the male in control of his future wife's behavior.

"I see." And Father Coyne was silent for a full minute. Then he said, "If she's domiciled in Dublin you won't need *my* permission." His stiff, formal tone had the subtle nuance of dignity wounded but unbowed.

"I'm awful sorry about this, Father," Timmy was saying. "If it was—" when he was interrupted by loud cheering and handclapping. Father O'Brien and family had arrived.

"Eight o'clock will be time enough," Nellie O'Brien had told her restive son earlier in the evening. "We're expected to be fashionably late." He felt better after his two-hour nap and, with scruples in abeyance for the time being, was looking forward to another round of pleasant adulation by friends and neighbors and parishioners at large. He was good at mingling and small talk, and this reception was the perfect occasion for him. He went from table to table, group to group, shook hands, blessed, chatted, laughed, and joked, enjoying in the process a little earthly reward for his years of sacrifice. Until he ran into Timmy Mulligan.

"Father O'Brien," said Timmy expansively. "'Tis well you're looking. And you'll give me your blessing, won't you? I couldn't make it to the mass in the morning. Business, you know." And he knelt there and then on the dusty floor of the parish hall.

Phelim was experiencing more than pure spiritual uplift as he raised his hands above Timmy Mulligan. To have the richest man in South Mayo kneel before him

God's

Anointed

221

said something for the kind of power with which he had been invested. "It's good to see you, Timmy," he said, helping him to his feet.

"A word in your ear now, Father. If we can talk in a quiet place." This was it, Phelim thought, as he followed him to the same corner of the hall where Mulligan had recently led Father Coyne. Money for the missions, for sure. He'd be off to Africa in a year, and it was not un-usual for people to give donations at ordination to help young missionaries on their way. A generous contribu-tion might be expected from one with this man's wealth. "I have a favor to ask," said Timmy in a very low voice.

"Certainly!" A request for a favor preceding the grant-ing of one.

"I'm getting married."

"Congratulations, Timmy. That's grand."

"And we'd like you to do the wedding."

"Well!" Wait till his mother heard about this! "Of course! I'd be delighted. Thank you for asking me." It would be his very first wedding too. "Do I know the lucky woman?"

"'Tis someone you know quite well indeed." Timmy was looking over his shoulder into the distance.

"Ah! Good! Good! That'll make it all the more de-lightful."

"It's Catherine Ryan." Timmy had refocused onto Phelim's chin.

"Well, for God's sake!" The exclamation spluttered autonomically out of him. "Catherine!" He could never after decide if his initial reaction was a cry of anguish or of mere surprise.

"She asked especially for you to do it."

His brain, his emotions, his stomach were all splashing around in the inside of his mother's churn. Catherine! *His* Catherine! She was no such thing anymore: he had settled that definitively last summer. It took a three-day private retreat and a general confession, but he did it. And that was that! But marrying Timmy Mulligan of the hooked nose and endless money? So? She was free, wasn't she? He had made *his* choice, now she was making hers. He had had his chance: she had, for God's sake, as good as asked him last summer, and he had turned her down. And hadn't regretted it since for one instant. By God, no! And never would again. So what was he disturbed about now? He wasn't! He couldn't be. And he wouldn't be.

"You'll do it, then?" Hard to tell whether that was fear or hope in Mulligan's voice.

He hesitated for a long minute. "No." Knowing, as he said it, that it was not a conscious decision: some grace or wisdom or perspicacity deep in his unconscious brain had made the choice for him and then left it to mere consciousness to justify or rationalize. "I wouldn't be able to get the time off. I still have a year of theological studies to complete, you see." Two statements, lie and truth, neatly combined to cover his retreat.

"That's too bad, now." But there was no mistaking the relief in Timothy Mulligan's voice. "I know Catherine will be awfully sorry to hear you can't do it."

Timmy's smugness would have dissipated had he been privy to the conversation that took place a few afternoons later between Eileen Laffey and Maura Higgins. Eileen couldn't wait to get over and chew the fat with her old friend. And when the discussion got around, as it soon did, to the impending nuptials of Mulligan and Catherine Ryan, Maura's immediate caustic comment was, "Second best for both of them, of course."

"What in God's name got into Catherine at all?" Eileen asked. The day was warm and they were sitting out in the back yard. "At least I had the excuse of being poor."

"Phelim O'Brien got into her, that's what." Maura sipped her sherry and nodded meaningfully. "In more ways than one, if you know what I mean."

"You can't be serious, Maura! Phelim is a holy man, for God's sake. Hasn't he just been ordained!" But you could see she was titillated all the same.

"All I can tell you is that his holiness didn't prevent a certain event from taking place last summer in Catherine Ryan's house. Which Catherine had hoped would get him out of the seminary and permanently into her bed. But it didn't anyway."

"And you're saying that's why she settled for Timmy?" Eileen's eyes were wide. "Faith, he must have lowered his standards too: when he was courting me he said he'd only marry a virgin."

"I'm told he hasn't changed his standards a bit." And Maura Higgins put back her head and laughed till the tears were streaming down her face. Eileen stared at her in bewilderment at first, then gradually joined in the merriment till she too was out of control.

"What are we laughing at anyway?" she managed at one stage.

Maura laughed even harder at that. Eventually she said, drying her eyes with her fingers, "We're laughing at stupidity and innocence and deceit and greed and hope and despair; all the things that make life worth-while. Here, have some more sherry." She stretched for the bottle.

"But," said Eileen, "Timmy obviously knows Catherine is not a virgin." She reached out her glass.

"Now, this is hard to believe," Maura said, with difficulty holding back the laughter again, "but so is the gullibility of man. Catherine has convinced that poor rich slob, Timmy Mulligan, that old Thomas Ryan was never able to perform what the clergy describe as consummation of their union and that there has been no one else in her love life. Never mind poor Reddy Ryan, that every goddamn eejit in the parish knew about, or Phelim O'Brien, or God knows who she carried on with in London, and I happen to know from herself that there were several."

"Can you believe it! Could the Timmy I nearly married really be that green?"

"Timmy believes what Timmy wants to believe, and Catherine set her cap at him when Phelim turned her down, and she has money now and brains of a sort and a certain sophistication that our simple lad from Creevagh just couldn't resist."

Sheep bleated in a nearby field. Cart wheels crunched the gravel road. On the quiet evening air the sound of the Angelus bell drifted past. The two women sipped their sherry in silence.